The Allure of a Predator

Charles Richardson

www.seraphbooks.com

Cover Design By: Alyssa M. Curry
Copyediting: Alyssa M. Curry
Cover Photo: Kevin Sebastian

ISBN Paperback: 978-1-941711-07-1
ISBN E-Book: 978-1-941711-08-8
Library of Congress Control Number: 2014957426

For information regarding special discounts for bulk purchases of this book for educational, gift purposes, as a charitable donation, or to arrange a speaking event, please visit: www.seraphbooks.com

www.charleshrichardson.com
twitter@Chaz6262
www.facebook.com/charles.h.richardson2

Dedication

To my parents, Charles and Rose, who taught me the value of integrity, hard work, and perseverance.

As well, I dedicate this book to my wife, Rosalyn, brother, Randy, my children, Tiombe, Dequan, Chaz and granddaughter, Velene. Thank you to my in-laws, Mom and Dad Fair, Bennie, and Isaac.

Special persons – Sylvia, Lena, Gwen, Linda, Paula, and Kamilah. All of my family and loved ones who have supported this project, Pastor Charles L. Wheeler, and my Mountaintop Missionary Baptist Church family.

Thank You and God Bless!

Acknowledgements

This book would not have been written without the assistance and guidance of my Copyeditor, Cover Designer and Caramel Angel, Alyssa M. Curry. I want to thank her for helping me organize my words with the creativity and skill that brought my journey to fruition.

I want to express a special thank you to Marala Scott and my dear friend for her encouragement and support throughout the years.

Finally, I want to thank Seraph Books for granting me the opportunity to publish this book.

Introduction

When you consider the image of a predator, it would not include an attractive woman, driving an upscale automobile, who lives in an exclusive gated community with two beautiful children. At least that was not James' perception. He considered himself to be an intelligent, well-educated, successful businessman from the East Coast. He thought he had been exposed to most personality types that allowed him to avoid potentially harmful associations or relationships.

The Allure of a Predator is based on true events. It involved an unsuspecting and obviously naïve person being lured into a marriage under false pretenses. They say hindsight is 20/20 and in James' case, that was absolutely true. There were signals and red flags that he refused to acknowledge during his relationship that should have prevented him from going forward. The purpose of this book is to help unsuspecting victims to avoid predicaments like these or worse.

The subject of people being victimized by predators and con artists has been a serious topic for a while. We have read real stories or watched television shows showing how predators single out individuals. They convince the victim that they love them and can have a wonderful life together.

Although this story may bring back painful memories to victims, this book is written to warn others how easily one can fall victim to someone like Marlene who created a marriage filled with turmoil, financial bondage, mental anguish and regret. However, when James accepted the fact that adversity makes you stronger and more faithful, he knew God meant the experience for good. Now you must share the story so it may help the abuser and abused to acknowledge the impious nature of their behavior and seek help from a trained professional practitioner in mental health.

If this has happened to you, you are not alone. It is our hope and prayer that this book will warn and encourage others to avoid people whose ultimate goal is to take advantage of you and make your self-worth and self-preservation your top priority. Predators are out there looking for their next victim. So beware, do not ignore the red flags or be blinded by *The Allure of a Predator.*

Chapter 1

East Coast to West Coast

It's funny how your past follows you for the rest of your life. You don't have to live in it, but it's there; especially if you don't make good decisions when you know something doesn't seem right. Well, I knew and I disregarded what God was telling me because I wanted what I had in front of me. In fact, no one could have told me differently. I felt a queasiness rise up from my stomach while a light covering of perspiration formed above my brow. I walked into the room and sat down at the large conference table with a black tape recorder, video recorder, yellow notepad, pen and two glasses resting on it. After the court reporter, videographer, and index of exhibits were placed on the record, I was sworn in as a witness. Afterwards, the attorney began.

"Good morning Mr. Fairchild. Are you ready?" the gentleman asked.

"Um. Just one moment please," I said taking a deep breath as I unbuttoned my blue suit jacket. May I?" I asked reaching for the water pitcher.

"Help yourself."

I picked up the pitcher of ice water, filled the glass in front of me, and took a couple of sips. He nodded his head and I replied with the same. He pressed play and began asking a barrage of questions. I never thought I'd be here, but given my situation, who would? Although he had a lot of questions, there would surely be many he knew nothing about. No one could disseminate the lies and evil, which manifested inside a predators mind because it ran too deep. I looked towards the windows displaying a perfect view of the city and allowed my recollections to return.

After graduating from a prestigious New England area business school, I was well trained to present a detailed report on my company's West Coast operations. I worked in the controller's office on the same floor as our CEO and president. My responsibilities included preparation of monthly financial statements for our West Coast media outlet, located in Los Angeles. These were acquisitions made within the last twelve months and the company was still evaluating their performance. Based upon the financials, they weren't doing well.

On a Thursday afternoon, I saw Mr. Thompson, CEO/President, heading to his office and asked him if he had a minute to speak. He was sharply dressed and returning from a meeting. I knew once he reached his desk, he wouldn't have time for me. The corporate headquarters was structured and although Mr. Thompson was cordial to me, I should have requested a formal meeting with his secretary. However, I took the opportunity to catch him in the hallway to ask him for a quick meeting. He agreed and as we walked by his secretary's desk, I could feel her piercing eyes as she mumbled to herself, "What is *he* doing here?" Mrs. Jones was typically nice to me, but protective of the President.

The meeting was brief and to the point. I told Mr. Thompson I was aware that he had been disappointed with the results from our West Coast operation. Further, since I communicated with their staff on a regular basis and prepared their financials, I had suggestions and recommendations that would improve results.

Showing a genuine curiosity he asked, "You do? What are they?"

"I would rather present a formal report for your review. It'll detail my thoughts and recommendations."

"Great. I look forward to receiving the report."

Around ten the next morning, Mrs. Jones called and said the president wanted to see me. As I walked to his office, I wondered if he changed his mind about my report. Perhaps I had overstepped my boundary in speaking with him yesterday. I felt a bit nervous entering his office until I noticed that he had a smile on his face. He asked me to give him my report. Surprised and happy he hadn't changed his mind, I told him, "Certainly. It'll be a detailed report and I plan to complete it over the weekend."

"Oh, okay. So you will have it for me next week?" he asked as he tapped his hand on his desk two times.

"Yes. I'll have it to you on Monday," I assured him.

As I left his office, I felt he appreciated that I'd work on the report over the weekend instead of on company time. The pressure was on. Mr. Thompson seemed interested in the report, so I knew it had to be both impressive and actionable.

I had just received my masters degree two months earlier so I was still in my term paper, thesis-writing mode. I knew I was up for the challenge, based upon my education and handling the West Coast records.

Over a twelve-hour period, I was able a complete a ten-page document inclusive of my recommendations that would improve operation effectiveness, efficiencies, and overall staff evaluation. We had a successful operation at corporate, so many of our suggestions were already tested and working well. The major concern I addressed involved the lack of our corporate controls and culture in the facilities outside of our East Coast headquarters. My final recommendation stated the need for an onsite internal audit, conducted by our company controller. I felt that this audit would confirm my assessment of their operations and implement changes needed to improve results on the West Coast.

While I was preparing the report, I thought about the politics of presenting my analysis directly to the president of the company. At the time, I was the assistant controller for the West Coast. Therefore, my direct supervisor was the corporate controller and above him were the vice president and general manager. My intent was never to disrespect them by going over their heads or neglecting to share my ideas. When I arrived to the office on Monday, I made sure I spoke with them about my report prepared for the president. They thanked me for giving them a heads up, but both said I should have spoken to them before Mr. Thompson. Then I called Mrs. Jones to inform her that I had something to present to the president. I was at my desk for about an hour before

Mrs. Jones called to let me know that Mr. Thompson was ready.

My meeting went well. He asked me to present the report orally, covering each point and recommendations. He asked a lot of questions as the report covered personnel, accounting, and sales. A major concern was the level of trade and barter transactions used each month. The president thanked me for the report and appreciated my concern regarding the company's financial health at our new facility. In addition, he said he'd share the report with corporate management and the board of directors. Needless to say, I was quite impressed with myself. I humbly thanked Mr. Thompson for his time and the opportunity to present my report. Then I returned to my work.

Although my title was assistant controller, before my report to the president, I was considered a glorified bookkeeper. However, after my presentation, I was viewed in a different light. I was now invited to all management meetings, as well as, meetings with the financial institutions that financed our West Coast acquisitions. Two weeks after receiving my report, the president shared the information with the board of directors. The results of the meeting included the decision to send the controller to do the audit I recommended. Two days after, he was on his way to California.

The controller spent about eight days conducting the audit and interviewing staff. He called me a few times during his visit asking specific questions regarding issues raised in my report. He told me that my findings were accurate and in fact, corporate must have a sense of urgency on getting these issues resolved. Upon his return to the home office, he met with Mr. Thompson, the general manager and me to discuss the results.

He reported that changes had to be made at the highest level of management and there were few members of the staff we could trust. The person he had the most confidence in was the office manager. Her name was Nancy Arnett and she was basically running the day-to-day operations because the general manager was rarely in the office. I'd spoken to Nancy several times over the months and she seemed to know what was going on at the company. However, I felt she had limited skills regarding her specific job of handling the traffic department. Traffic was directly related to the sales department and was vital to the company's profitably. At the conclusion of the meeting, it was determined that we have to quickly develop a strategy for implementation at our West Coast property.

It was late fall and six weeks after my initial review when the vice president approached me on a Wednesday afternoon.

"How do you like California?" she asked.

"I don't know. I've never been there but I heard it's a nice place to visit."

She smiled and said, "Well, make plans to visit because we need you there on Friday."

"Wow! Really?"

"Yes. Mrs. Jones is making your travel arrangements as we speak."

My mind was spinning. I knew the controller's report wasn't complete and another visit was necessary, but I thought he'd make the return visit. I guess because of my hands-on experience working with the company, I was the ideal candidate to complete our evaluation. I was told that they needed me there for one month. I had to get my personal affairs in order, pack, and be ready to go on Friday afternoon. I was single at the time, so getting packed and handling my personal business was easy.

The flight to California was comfortable. I had reservations about being on a five-hour flight, since an hour was the longest time I'd spent on a plane. In addition, the furthest point west I'd ever been was New Jersey. Prior to my trip, I made arrangements for the local sales manager, Mike Turner, to meet me at the airport. Upon arrival at LAX, I was able to spot Mike right away based on his description. The plan was to get me checked into my hotel and drive over to the office for a brief tour. It was two West Coast time. I had about two hours for the tour and an informal meet-and-greet with the staff.

The general manager was out of town but expected to return to the office on Monday. He was the source behind many of the issues we were facing. The weather was perfect. The drive from the hotel to the office only took five minutes. The office was housed in a small two-story building, which was a far cry from our thirty-floor office building that our headquarters were located in. We occupied five floors. This was only the first of many differences between their facilities and the home office.

The tour was quick, however, the staff meeting lasted longer than expected. My intent was to say hello and let them know I'd return on Monday to conduct individual meetings with each staff member. Nancy, the office manager, was eager to meet me and asked a lot of questions. In most cases, I couldn't give her detailed answers. She seemed overly anxious and inquired as to why I was there, since the controller recently conducted an internal audit.

My meeting was with a group of twenty employees and I could tell they were nervously waiting to find out what was next. A couple of people asked questions, but Nancy dominated the conversation. I remembered the controller mentioned Nancy was the one person he trusted. I thought she was aggressive based on her relationship with the controller. After the meeting, I told both Mike and Nancy, I would be working on company business over the weekend. I wanted to meet them on Saturday for lunch to discuss some concerns I had. Mike had a prior commitment, but Nancy was able to meet with me at noon. I had questions for her based upon her reports on sales results and decided to use this meeting as our one-on-one session originally scheduled for next week.

Nancy arrived right on time and we had lunch in the hotel restaurant. We started with a casual conversation about her background and being a native Californian. I told her I was born and raised in D.C. and this was the furthest West I'd ever traveled. After the light chat, I commenced with business-related topics. She became a bit tense when I began to ask specific questions about her traffic department and allocation of trade expenses. She stated that these matters were discussed during the first audit and she felt she had answered all of his questions. I assured her that she probably did answer all of his questions, but I had others.

At that point, she grew defensive and asked, "What other questions do you have? And do you think I'm doing anything wrong?"

I didn't think she was doing anything wrong although there were a couple of loose ends I needed to explore. I decided to cover general subjects regarding her department and speak with the general manager on Monday. Nancy appeared at ease when she was discussing other areas in the organization but became particularly negative on matters concerning the general manager. She mentioned his lack of presence in the office and his frequent trips out of town. Nancy noted the lack of commitment in the sales department, which included the local sales manager. I guess she was happy Mike couldn't make it. As we ended the meeting, she told me she had called the controller to ask why he wasn't coming back for the follow-up visit. She failed to tell me his response. I informed her since I handled West Coast financials, management felt I should make the next visit. We ended the conversation there but I told her I'd see her on Monday.

As I loosened my tie and headed back to my room, I didn't have a good feeling about Nancy. She was unusually guarded, defensive when discussing her responsibilities and too forthcoming when talking about personnel and departments other than hers. I had a lot to consider.

I spent the rest of the weekend studying material on company finances and administrative functions. I called Mike to tell him he didn't have to pick me up Monday morning; I rented a car from the hotel.

I arrived at nine in the morning and went directly to the general manager's office, Jerry Monahan. He had over twenty-five years of experience in the industry and we retained his services when we took over another office. Jerry was definitely old school. He did the whole three-martini lunch, sales department rules, and anything to get the sale. He always asked, "What's in it for me?" His employment background was checkered, to say the least. We were the sixth company he had worked for and the main reason we retained him was because we couldn't find a suitable replacement at the time we purchased the media company where he was employed.

Jerry greeted me with a big smile and firm handshake. Our meeting lasted more than an hour. We discussed poor sales results, personnel issues, unusual high use of trade and the amount of time he spends away from the office. Just like the office manager, he was defensive too. Although I asked tough questions, I didn't solicit them in a demeaning or disrespectful manner. However, my questions weren't sugarcoated and they required direct and honest answers. We needed a strong general manager in that position so reasonable and direct answers that made sense were all we needed. Jerry's responses included weak excuses, finger pointing at his staff, and lack of direction from headquarters. I told him that I corresponded with his organization on a weekly basis and this was the first time he'd ever requested help or direction from headquarters. Furthermore, I indicated since he had extensive experience with the company and region, we felt his leadership was needed for a successfully managed organization. As you can imagine, the meeting did not end well. I told Jerry I would be on-site for a few weeks to evaluate his operation and that the new group chairman would be joining me in two weeks. I left his office and went into a conference room to begin my one-on-one meeting with the staff.

In two days, I completed the meetings came to the conclusion that not only did we have a problem generating revenue, but there was a major personnel problem. The meetings were uncomfortable and awkward. The staff members didn't know me, so the conversations weren't as candid. I attempted to put them at ease and let them know that anything they shared with me would be confidential. I felt they didn't believe me or they feared repercussions once I completed my evaluation and returned to the home office. What I did determine was the organization needed a wholesale change in attitude from top to bottom. My feedback to corporate after one week on-site was that we needed to reorganize the management structure and some heads had to roll.

The new chairman was Mr. Thompson's eldest son. He was a corporate attorney with a large East Coast law firm. It was my understanding that he was in line for a partnership with the firm, but decided to join his father in his growing family business. His first name was Anthony; however everyone called him J.R. I met him a couple of times and he seemed to be a sharp and serious individual. I spent the following week formalizing and updating my recommendations based upon my observations. From my professional evaluation, what the company needed most was a new general manager. The current one was out of the office two days within my first week in town. I concluded that either he knew his days were numbered or he actually had another job. After our initial meeting on Monday, we had little contact. The office manager attempted to get in my good graces by offering a daily rundown of what was going on in the office. It was something she was good at; I only wished she performed her job as well. I'm certain that was the reason she gained the controller's trust during his visit; she was the local informant.

Mike, the local sales manager, was a nice guy. There were a couple of evenings that we went out for drinks after work. On Saturday, he drove me around town to see the sites. He was married with two children and made it known that he had a monthly mortgage of two thousand and eight hundred dollars. It was obvious he needed his job and made a point to make sure I enjoyed my stay in Los Angeles as much as possible. In our discussions, I was honest with him regarding the lack of production in the sales department. In addition, it was Mike's first management position and he was having a difficult time attracting qualified account executives. My opinion, which I kept to myself, was that in the pending reorganization, Mike could be retained as a senior account executive, not management.

I decided my mission during my initial meeting with J.R. was to clearly convey that we must hire winners. We needed people with positive attitudes who had the best interest of the organization first; which wasn't the case there. It seemed as though most of the staff had their own personal agendas, where they would benefit before all others, including the company. The most egregious violator of the company's philosophy was the general manager, Jerry Monahan.

I discovered there was wholesale abuse of barter or trade transactions at the company. There was more than a fair exchange of services between two companies; it should provide both marketing and financial benefits for both sides. We were providing our services to several vendors; however what we received, in most cases, were bonuses and perks for Jerry. I found evidence of Jerry using barter for family trips to Hilton Head, leasing a car for his wife, and maintenance agreements for landscaping, as well as, remodeling his home. He tried to hide the transactions as business-related expenses, but with a little digging, it became clear these transactions had nothing to do with business. I didn't confront Jerry with my findings because I wanted to discuss the situation with J.R. first. In addition, even if the general manager authorized the transactions, there were other staff members who had to know what he was doing was wrong. At that point, no one had come forward, not even Nancy Arnett.

On my trip to the airport to pickup the group chairman, I had to decide how and when I should present my analysis to him. I was sure J.R. had extensive information on the operation and me, so I decided to drive him to his hotel and begin the conversation over dinner. J.R. was staying at an upscale hotel located downtown. Our conversation from the airport was pleasant and light, which was a good start.

While I waited in the lobby for J.R., I looked over my presentation again. I had documents in my briefcase, but I didn't want to get too detailed over dinner. The formal meeting would take place the following Monday morning. During dinner, I did most of the talking. J.R. asked an occasional question, but he was focused on what I was sharing. Based upon his questions and facial expressions, I felt he was concerned and knew action needed to be taken. After dinner, we went to the hotel bar for a nightcap. He admitted that changes had to be made and he wanted to begin soon.

I spent my weekend developing a strategy for terminating and replacing the general manager. I felt he was a poor example of how to manage a successful business. He abused his authority and the staff could see his behavior on a consistent basis. Although J.R. didn't say it, I believed we needed to set the precedence; the general manager had to go. I was certain he'd agree. Jerry had a big personality and was probably well liked in the industry, but I didn't believe he was well respected as a business executive based upon his employment history. He couldn't get or keep a job. I learned that seemed to be the nature of that industry in upper management. The excellent executives are well compensated and rarely leave their jobs, while the Jerry Monahan's of the world are left playing musical chairs for other employment opportunities.

Dave Gifford, a staffing and recruiting consultant, has a formula. "Prevention! Detection! Correction!" He claimed it was the way to eliminate personnel problems. Going forward we must hire the right person for the right position. I knew we had no margin for error when hiring our next general manager. If we made the right hire, we would be able to attract a sales staff in particular, with winning and company first attitudes. I felt we detected the problem areas; we were ready to make corrections.

I arrived to the office at eight thirty that morning. I had been assigned a small office when I arrived two weeks ago. The office had two desks so I guessed J.R. would be sharing this space with me initially. When J.R. arrived, he asked for my location. He came to my office and we discussed how we should proceed. I suggested we have a brief meeting with the general manager and have him call a quick staff meeting to introduce J.R. as our new group chairman. Both J.R. and I knew this would be Jerry's last week for the company.

For the first time, Jerry was visibly nervous. He tried to put on a good front when he introduced J.R. to the staff. He even attempted to lighten the mood with a bad joke about J.R. coming directly from Dallas, referring to the television show.

J.R. was brief and stated, "As new owners, we want you to be a successful and important contributor to our corporation. We'll do everything in our power to get that done in short order."

The meeting was over in ten minutes and J.R. told Jerry we would like to meet with him. The meeting with Jerry was intense. He was presented with a list of abuses and mismanagement of company resources. As an attorney, J.R. was using legal language, which made Jerry even more nervous. At one point, Jerry asked if we wanted him to reimburse the company. J.R. responded that it wasn't the point, and the fact that he committed these misappropriations was problematic.

Prior to the meeting, J.R. and I decided our course of action would be to get as much information and details from Jerry and then terminate him on Friday. The key was to make him feel he had a chance for redemption by assisting us in identifying other areas of concerns I may have missed in my evaluation. Basically, we needed him to provide information on the office manager and the sales personnel that was detrimental to the operation; the strategy worked. He knew that Nancy was using barter transactions for personal use as well and the sales staff was inferior to their counterparts in the market place. Based upon the sales results or lack of shame, that was a no brainer. We fired Jerry at close of business on Thursday with no severance pay and cancellation of all ongoing trade agreements. This meant he was personally liable for his wife's auto lease payments, landscaping, and remodeling his house. He was relieved we weren't going to pursue legal action.

Our next step was to identify a potential general manager. I was pleased to hear that J.R.'s extensive network, which was nationwide, helped him obtain names of a few candidates for consideration. On Friday, J.R. wanted to have a corporate conference call. He didn't tell me the nature of the call, but I figured it would be a recap of events over the last three weeks and the plans going forward. During the meeting, I was asked if I wanted to permanently relocate to California as the regional director of operations and general manager. I was asked to fly home on the weekend and meet at the home office on Monday. J.R. would remain in L.A. to oversee operations until my situation was finalized and I was prepared to relocate.

On Monday morning, I arrived at the office at seven thirty. Mrs. Jones called to tell me President Thompson and the chairman of the board was ready to see me. Horace Walker, the board director, opened the meeting by praising me on the initial report I presented to the president. He stated I was doing an outstanding job out west. I thanked him and at that point, Mr. Thompson entered the discussion.

"Are you ready to relocate?"

"I definitely appreciate the opportunity, but it's a major decision." My two children and parents lived on the east coast and I needed to take that under consideration.

"I understand, but this is an opportunity of a lifetime. It would be financially worthwhile and your increased compensation would allow you to travel home at least once a month."

At the time, I had a good salary for an assistant controller at about sixty-five thousand annually. The chairman indicated that he knew my current salary and the board had agreed to double my compensation. I would be provided with a company car and an expense account. I tried to remain cool, but I must admit, I almost fell out of my chair. When I regained my composure, I thanked them again and said, "This is a very generous offer, and I accept."

Like *The Godfather*, they made me an offer I couldn't refuse. Mr. Thompson told me to go home right away and begin preparation to leave to assume my new position. He added, "We need you there in one week, so make it happen!" I left the office with my head spinning; I had so much to do and so little time to do it.

I knew the company had a sense of urgency to get the West Coast operations on the right track, but one week was not nearly enough time to relocate. I was a divorced father of two and managed to have a civil relationship with my ex-wife. She was surprised I was relocating and was concerned about our kids. My daughter was eleven years old and my son was five at the time. I was close to my children and we spent time together at least once a week. That would be the hardest adjustment I'd have to make.

Much to my surprise, I was able to close my business affairs within the week. I called Mrs. Jones to make travel arrangements and told her I wanted to leave early Sunday morning, so I could be at the office first thing Monday. My family threw me a surprise going away party that Saturday, which was both joyful for the wonderful opportunity and painful for having to leave my children, family, and friends. I knew the additional income would enable me to come home on a monthly basis; however, the various problems that still needed to be addressed out west wouldn't allow me to make frequent trips back home.

I used the five-hour flight to L.A. to map out a strategy for transforming the staff. The most important hire would be a high profile and respected media executive as our new general manager. The person must be well known in the L.A. market and have the ability to recruit the best and brightest sales and administrative personnel. J.R. received some recommendations for candidates through his contact. After reviewing them there were two people who, on paper, fit that description. The challenge would be convincing them to join a company based on the East Coast with minimal market presence in L.A., while meeting their salary demands. We needed to determine how we could attract a person who was well established in the L.A. market. The answer was simple. We needed to make them an offer they couldn't refuse. I knew it could be done because they had just done it with me. We would be considered a start up situation, so the offer needed to be compelling and it involve more than a big paycheck.

I called J.R. when I checked into my hotel to see how things were going and I wanted to share ideas about upgrading the personnel. He agreed to meet me for breakfast Monday morning before going to the office. During breakfast, J.R. mentioned that he had an incident with Nancy involving a missing bank deposit. The deposit was found the next day; however, he felt there was something strange about the entire episode. We agreed she was the next person we had to replace.

Things were quiet at the office. Roughly an hour after I arrived, the office manager asked if she could speak with me in the conference room. I told her that would be fine and I'd meet her in five minutes. She was almost in tears when she entered the conference room.

"What's wrong?"

"I'm upset with Mr. Thompson Jr." She felt he accused her of stealing money while I was away and the deposit was simply misplaced. I told her J.R. told me about the incident and it was just a misunderstanding. I didn't tell her J.R. believed she was attempting to steal the deposit and the only reason it was found the next day was because she got caught. I encouraged Nancy to continue working hard and everything would be okay, but this was far from the truth.

J.R. was leaving on Wednesday, so we spent the next day and a half researching candidates for the general manager position. We discovered the task would be more difficult than we thought. The best candidate was not interested in having an exploratory conversation with us and the other was so vested in his company's pension program that he would lose money if he left. J.R. decided to discuss the matter with his father and develop the best possible compensation package we could offer candidates. He told me to be prepared to handle the acting general manager responsibilities longer than we anticipated because he didn't want to settle.

It may sound too simplistic, but most growing businesses seldom hire the best people. Instead, they settle and hire someone who is available; a prime example was our company retaining Jerry Monahan, the former general manager. J.R. didn't want to make any more bad hire's just because the person was available and willing to work for a start-up organization.

Quite honestly, I wasn't qualified to be the general manager of a challenged media company. I had great exposure working at headquarters and saw how a strong organization should operate. Furthermore, Rose Tyce, our East Coast vice president and general manager was only a phone call away if I ran into any situation and needed advice. What I had going for me was the strong financial and management experience I gained as an operating management executive, a position I held prior to joining Ascending Media Group. My focus was on administration and finance, as well as working closely with Mike Turner and the sales staff. I knew the key to sales was to hold them accountable and make sure they were prospecting, making calls, and getting appointments everyday.

J.R. called me a few days later, informing me that the board agreed to develop an aggressive compensation deal. At least it would attract enough interest that prospects would agree to meet with us. He asked me to get his tape recorder out of the safe and mail it to him so he can have Mrs. Jones transcribe the recordings.

I called a staff meeting the following Monday. I told them, "The present situation will make unusual demands on all of us, but knowing you as I do, I'm confident that we are equal to the challenge." I wasn't convinced, but we had to attempt to build the staff's self-confidence and improve company moral. After the meeting, Nancy told me that was the best staff meeting she has attended since she joined the company. She claimed she was inspired. If she only knew we were on to her.

I went to retrieve J.R.'s tape recorder but when I opened the safe, the recorder wasn't there. As Nancy was about to leave for the day, I asked, "Have you seen the group chairman's tape recorder in the safe?"

She was the only person other than J.R. and me to have the combination to the safe; therefore, she was the only person to have access.

She replied coyly, "No, I haven't seen the recorder. J.R. probably just misplace it."

"Okay, I'll let him know."

I couldn't help but to think Nancy stole J.R.'s tape recorder. I called J.R. to tell him his recorder wasn't in the safe and Nancy's reply. J.R. asked me why Nancy was involved since she told him she didn't know the combination to the safe on a day he needed access. I informed J.R. that Alex Gared, our corporate controller told me he gave the office manager the combination when he was there for the internal audit.

J.R. was upset and snapped, "That woman stole my recorder and it has sensitive information on it! Call the police and make a report. I need my tape recorder and she has it!"

After I called the police, all hell broke out because Nancy wouldn't go quietly. Through my interaction and observation of her character, I knew she was a fighter and would try to lie her way out of any situation. The police dispatcher answered and after I stated the reason for my call, she transferred me to Detective Blackwell. I told the detective I was James Fairchild, the general manager at Ascending Media Group West. I explained we were in transition regarding company operations and personnel and had cause to believe there was a serious issue with employee theft. Our former general manager was terminated for that reason, along with his behavior, which was observed by many of the staff. The latest incident involved the theft of our group chairman's personal and expensive tape recorder.

"Are you suspicious of anyone in particular?" Detective Blackwell asked.

"Yes, her name is Nancy Arnett. She's the office manager. I questioned her about the missing recorder and she denied any knowledge of the item. She suggested that the chairman probably misplaced it." I informed the detective of other examples of theft of products and services, and that the local sales manager told me, "If it's not nailed down, it'll be missing the next morning." I knew we had a serious problem. After completing his report, Detective Blackwell said he would like to visit the office and interview a few of our employees, including Ms. Arnett.

Blackwell arrived at ten the next morning and from a list of employees he requested, he selected six staff members to interview, which included Nancy Arnett and Mike Turner, the local sales manager. He took about two hours to complete his interviews and determined that Nancy had major discrepancies in her responses. He felt it was serious enough to request a court ordered search warrant to examine her home. Upon completion of the police search, Detective Blackwell called and said her home was stocked like a warehouse. They found office supplies and equipment, a telephone system that accommodated six telephones, and an expensive tape recorder. He said, "It probably belongs to your boss. I'm sure we have enough evidence for an arrest of Ms. Arnett." I began a policy of cross training among the staff so the assistant traffic manager could take over office management duties once Nancy was terminated. She was arrested and charged with suspicion of theft of merchandise and services. On

Saturday, she was sent a registered letter of termination the next business day.

The case took six months to go to trial and business had to continue. A positive event occurred during our search for a general manager. Approximately, a month into our search, we received a call from a gentleman named Jeffrey Silver. Jeffrey was a highly respected media executive, who spent most of his career in California. For the past five years, he was working with a large media company located on the East Coast. He told J.R. and me that he was in town on leave from his company, to care for his elderly parents. Jeffrey, being their only child, felt it was his responsibility to provide that support, not only financially, but physically. Our search was being conducted privately through J.R.'s media network so the call from Mr. Silver was a pleasant surprise. It was unfortunate regarding his personal situation; however, we could provide him with an outstanding employment opportunity and the ability to be close to his parents.

After two interviews and an extensive background search, we offered Jeffrey the newly created vice president, general manager position. His compensation package included a high six-figure salary, bonus incentives on growth in revenue, and corporate stocks options. Personally, I felt he wanted to return home, so we didn't have to present such an expensive package. However, Mr. Thompson, J.R., and the chairman of the board felt a well respected and experienced executive like Jeffrey was an investment worth making. They believed he would attract qualified sales staff and generate business because of his affiliation with our company. They were absolutely right. Soon after, we were considered major players in the L.A. market.

Looking back on the decision, it was apparent. He was able to attract an outstanding sales manager from one of the top media companies in the market. In return, the sales manager brought two of his best account executives. Although Mike Turner was retained as an account executive, he lost his sales manager title. Only one other sales person was kept from the former sales team.

J.R.'s visits became less frequent. He was spending more time at headquarters with his father, planning future acquisitions. Locally, business was turning around and I was having success in upgrading the administrative and support staff. However, I always had the time bomb that was the pending Nancy Arnett trial in the back in my mind. I received feedback that Nancy and two other former female salespersons were considering wrongful termination legal actions pending the outcome of the trial.

One week before Nancy Arnett's trial, I received a call from the district attorney's office. The assistant district attorney told me he would be calling me to testify and asked if I'd come in to discuss the case. The next day I met him in his office. He assured me the case against Ms. Arnett was strong and he was confident we would get a conviction. The trial was scheduled for the following Tuesday morning at nine. Upon my arrival, I was surprised to see it would be a jury trial. The ADA informed me that I would be his second witness, after Detective Blackwell's testimony. I was called to the stand about an hour later. I was nervous initially, but as my testimony proceeded, I became more comfortable. However, my comfort level dissipated when the cross-examination began. She was a female attorney and I could not believe the questions she began asking me.

"Mr. Fairchild, didn't you authorize Ms. Arnett to have the company supplies and equipment to be shipped to her home since your company had limited storage space?"

"No. It is my understanding that the material was ordered and delivered prior to me relocating to California and we have plenty of storage space at the office."

"Weren't you in charge of West Coast operations while working in your D.C. office, so you could have authorized the purchases from there?"

"I handled the preparation of their financial statement; I was not authorized to approve purchases which is the former general manager's responsibility."

"So the former general manager could have authorized these transactions and storage arrangements?"

"I spoke to the former general manager when missing supplies were discovered during our company's internal audit. He said, 'I don't know anything about missing supplies or equipment.'"

"I understand that general manager was terminated. What was the reason? Was it theft of services and equipment?"

"No, it was for poor performance." The next question was mind-blowing and displayed the deceit and level of lies Nancy Arnett would tell to save herself by any means necessary.

"Isn't it true that the real reason Ms. Arnett was terminated was because she refused sexual advances by you?"

"No, absolutely not! She was terminated because the L.A. Police Department found our company's supplies and equipment in her home and they determined that material was stolen by Ms. Arnett!"

I was on the stand for two hours and re-examined by the ADA to establish that I had an outstanding employment record and no history of any wrongdoing. Further, I was promoted and sent to Ascending Media Group West due to my excellent job performance. His examination made me feel better. However, it would take some time for me to recover from the defense attorney's cross-examination. Nancy Arnett was a horrible human being and I didn't like her attorney either.

The trial ended after the defense called two character witnesses to testify on Nancy's behalf. Both were relatives, I think they were her cousins. The jury received their instructions and left the courtroom to begin deliberations. I returned to the office and spent the rest of the day wondering what happened. I received a call from the DA's office at eleven the next morning. He told me the jury had reached their verdict and much to his surprise, they found her "not guilty". I was at a complete loss as to how that could happen. He said he thought the jury felt sorry for her. Although the former general manager stole services and merchandise, he was not arrested. He said Ms. Arnett listened to the group chairman's tape recordings and although we didn't officially fire him for stealing, the tapes probably proved otherwise. The jury saw this big, bad corporation against a woman who was now unemployed. The DA concluded the jury couldn't send her to jail. I was devastated. I hung up the phone, leaned back in my chair, and sat in my office completely stunned. I decided to call J.R. to give him the bad news and he was shocked by the verdict too.

"It's obvious the DA mishandled the case," he huffed. "The tape recordings weren't admissible and should not have been considered in the jury's deliberation. I'm calling that DA. Do you have the phone number?"

I gave him the number realizing that Nancy Arnett and her cohorts would be a thorn in my side for some time to come. And I was right!

I was genuinely troubled by how a person could be so deceitful. I'm not a perfect person to say the least, but the level of dishonesty exhibited by Nancy was unbelievable. I did some research and found an article by a licensed clinical social worker, Kristina Randle, Ph.D. She claimed, "Lying can be associated with certain personality disorders, though not always. The difference depends on why someone is lying." In my experience, non-personality disorder based lying is done for a purpose. Typically, it's to make someone appear to be better in some way. That type of lying is often tied to a self-image problem.

Alternatively, individuals who have personality disorders such as narcissistic personality disorder or antisocial personality disorder often lie for the purpose of manipulation. Individuals with narcissistic or antisocial disorders may lie because they can. I am not a psychologist; however, my experience with Nancy Arnett took lying and manipulating people to another level. I hoped I would not meet anyone else like that nor would I wish it on anyone.

The Allure of a Predator

Chapter 2

The Predator & the Prey

My social life was non-existent in the year I relocated to Los Angeles. I'd been out socially about eight times. That included hanging out with J.R. for dinner and drinks. One weekend, I was invited to Betty Winston's home with Mary Hallums for brunch. They were employees at the time and felt I needed a chance to experience something other than hotel or restaurant food. After four months of hotel living, I was pleased when I found a nicely furnished loft apartment downtown.

I had a good time at Betty's brunch. The conversation was casual and didn't involve much talk about work. Betty and Mary were account executives under the former management structure. Due to their limited experience and lackluster sales production, they didn't make the cut once our new management team came on board. They felt I should have given them more support when the decision was made to let them go. I told them that the new sales manager made that decision and I wasn't a part of the process, other than processing the final paperwork. They were nice ladies, or so I thought, but their sales productivity was lacking. I told them I was sorry, but I would be happy to write personal letters of recommendations on their behalf. They thanked me, so I felt we parted on good terms. Little did I know, they were friends with Nancy Arnett. Much to my regret, after they were terminated, the company discovered several bogus sales orders submitted by Betty and Mary, which were processed by Nancy Arnett. In an effort to clean up our accounts, we found those transactions were never authorized or signed by the clients indicated on the sales orders.

The general manager and I shared the same secretary. Our receptionist never returned after a national record promoter invited her to lunch. We were worried initially, but we heard the promoter offered her the dream job. I was surprised when she failed to give her notice because she was quite professional as our receptionist. Her new job included traveling and interaction with recording artists.

Nonetheless, we needed a receptionist. I told my secretary, Helen, we should recruit a person who was more mature and had a stable employment history. Without any notice, she informed me that she thought she'd found a suitable replacement. The individual was in the lobby waiting to be interviewed.

"Helen, you know I have a report due to corporate by tomorrow. I don't have time to interview anyone. Ask Jeff to do it."

"Mr. Silver is out of the office. He had a meeting to attend. Can you at least meet the woman and maybe we can re-schedule the interview?"

Reluctantly, I went to the lobby to meet the candidate. As I approached the woman in the chair, she lifted her head to meet my gaze and my heart stopped. She was strikingly beautiful and could easily turn heads when she entered any room. She was 5'6", had a fair complexion with long ebony hair. Her appearance and athletic figure would remind people of current television personality, singer and songwriter, Nicole Scherzinger. She stood and introduced herself.

"You're here to interview for our receptionist position, correct?"

"Yes and here's my résumé," she said offering it to me.

"Let's go upstairs and talk."

As we passed Helen's desk, I read her lips, "I thought you had a report to do?" I smiled and continued into the conference room.

Her name was Marlene Hughes; she was dressed in a blue pinstriped, fitted business suit. Based upon her résumé and appearance, she was overqualified for a receptionist position. She had extensive experience as a marketing consultant and worked independently for some major companies.

"Why would you want to work at such an entry-level position?"

"I'm in my final year of a program and I want a stress-free position so I can focus on school. Besides, I've heard a lot of good things about the company."

The interview lasted over an hour and I was impressed with her presentation. Although the receptionist was an entry-level position, it was an important position in any organization. The receptionist was the first person the outside world meets or hears when they reach our company, in person or by telephone. I was okay with the fact that she was overqualified for the position. At the conclusion of the interview, I asked Ms. Hughes if she would provide three references and she agreed. She thanked me for the interview and my secretary walked her out. Needless to say, she was hired the next day and began work the following Monday.

It was a month after Nancy was found not guilty, when I received a call from our corporate attorney. She informed me that the company had just received a complaint from the Equal Employment Opportunity Commission (EEOC) and the California Department of Fair Employment. The complaints filed on the behalf of Nancy Arnett, Mary Hallums, and Betty Winston alleged employment and sexual discrimination. The corporate attorney informed me that she was familiar with these former employees and the recently concluded trial. However, she needed to speak with J.R. and me to get further details and submit our response. I found out that I was specifically named in the complaint. I cannot say I was surprised with the turn of events, but it still hurt that the women would pursue such action.

Brenda Burns, the corporate attorney, flew out to California to meet and gather any and all of the information on these women. More importantly, she wanted my side of the story regarding their sexual harassment claims. I told her about the Saturday brunch, which was the only social contact I had with Ms. Hallums or Ms. Winston, and I never had any social interaction with Ms. Arnett. Ms. Burns submitted our response to the complaints. Approximately three months later, after a complete investigation, the claims were dismissed by both agencies as having no merit. I was pleased about the results, but these women were not finished. They were trying to destroy me.

The first two weeks on the job were uneventful for Marlene Hughes. Though she was quite popular with the male staff. She was invited to lunch everyday and on two occasions, she accepted. The first time was with the general manager and the other was with the sales manager. They both liked her and after speaking with her over lunch, felt she was an excellent hire. My first non-business encounter with her was unplanned. One day, I asked her if she had seen Jeff Silver.

"He left the office for a lunch meeting."

"Oh. He was supposed to drop me off at the car dealership to pick up my car. It was being serviced. I guess he forgot."

"I'm about to go to lunch; I can drop you off."

"No, that's alright. I don't want to interfere with your lunch hour."

"Don't worry about it. I don't use the entire hour anyway."

"Okay, if you don't mind. It's about fifteen minutes from here."

She was driving an older model of a light blue Jaguar. As I buckled in, I noticed she was pulling her loosely fitted, floral skirt above her knees.

She became aware of my gaze and claimed, "I like to be comfortable when I'm driving."

During the drive, she told me she really enjoyed the job and the people were kind. I asked about school and she said it was going well. I made her laugh when I told her about my challenge adjusting to the laid-back lifestyle in Los Angeles.

As we pulled into the parking lot of the driveway I said, "Thank you for the ride. I owe you lunch."

"I look forward to it."

A week later, I invited her to lunch. We talked about her work as a consultant and the professional athletes she worked with. She spoke lovingly about her children and invited me to her son's soccer game the following Saturday. She added that her son was an excellent athlete and I'd enjoy the playoff game. I wasn't a big soccer fan, but I thanked her for the invitation and said I'd let her know. At that point, we never discussed personnel matters other than our children and sports.

J.R. arrived the following week for one of his infrequent visits. He updated me on the progress of the EEOC complaint.

"Brenda Burns feels pretty good about the chances that the claim will be dismissed."

"That's good. There was nothing behind it but their lies. It's unfortunate the company had to deal with it."

"Corporate is pleased with the turn around of the West Coast and gave us kudos on hiring the new managers. Revenues are up and operating expenses are down so things are looking good. How's the new receptionist doing? She's a real looker," he added.

"She's professional and doing a good job."

I didn't tell him about her soccer game invitation. He spent the rest of his stay meeting with the new management and staff. He visited with friends on the weekend and was on a flight home Sunday night.

On Friday, Marlene asked if I was able to attend her son's game. I apologized for not getting back to her sooner and asked her for the location. She gave me the address and said she was hoping I'd make it. I was conflicted because I knew I wanted to see her outside of the office, but the EEOC claim was still pending, and it was a bad idea to socialize with any female employee. Since the game was being played at an open public soccer field, there would be plenty of witnesses. However, after experiencing the many lies and twisted events told by Nancy and her friends, one would be paranoid too. The naïve part of me decided it would be okay to attend the soccer game.

Surprisingly, it was an exciting soccer match. Marlene's son, Billy, was the best and fastest kid on the field. He scored all three of his team's goals and they won three to two. Billy was fourteen and already being recruited by high school football coaches in the area. Football was his best sport to play for the school. After the game, I met Billy and congratulated him. He humbly thanked me. I liked the way he carried himself and thought he was a fine young man. Marlene told me the team was going out for ice cream and I was welcome to come. Although I knew I had some time, I declined her offer. It didn't feel like the right thing to do. Consequently, I spent another boring weekend at home. L.A. was an exciting place with plenty of things to get into; I think I was still shell shocked from the court and the EEOC cases. Home alone was the best place for me to be at this time.

It was now four months since we hired Marlene and she asked if we could go to lunch.

"Is anything wrong?"

"No. I just want to run something by you outside of the office."

"Give me fifteen minutes and I'll meet you in the parking lot."

Before I could turn around, she blurted, "I've heard rumors about you and the company being sued for sexual harassment. I can't believe it," she said covering her mouth in dismay.

"It's a private matter and the corporation is handling it. I'm sorry but I can't discuss the matter with anyone."

"I just want you to know that my observation of your behavior, in and outside of the office, is exemplary. I know you're not capable of such a thing."

"I'm not perfect, but you're right, I wouldn't do that. People have their own agenda's and don't care who they hurt."

"Hey, let's talk about something a little more cheerful. I like playing racquetball. What about you?"

"I played tennis and a little handball back east when I was younger."

"What? You're still young. Do you want to learn how to play racquetball this weekend?"

I paused and then answered, "Yes, I would."

I was upset the staff was talking about the discrimination case and I was tired of staying home every weekend. I didn't ask Marlene who was discussing the case in the office, but I was going to speak with my administrative assistant on Monday.

Marlene was surprised how well I played racquetball for the first time. She beat me in all three games, but I was competitive. She was taking it easy at first, but when I started returning her serves consistently, she ramped up her game.

After the games, she asked, "Have you played before?"

"No. I developed my hand and eye coordination playing baseball from an early age through college. I got the same reaction when I started playing tennis a few years back."

"Well, you're a pretty good athlete. I have to tell Billy when I get home. What are you doing after this?"

"Nothing really. I'll probably grab something to eat."

"I'm hungry too. Let's go to lunch. I know a nice place you'll like and it has a great wine selection."

She was right, the food was good and the wine was wonderful. We spent over two hours laughing and talking about everything from politics and religion to sports. We had a great time, but I knew if we continued to have this much fun together, something would have to give, and it did.

I arrived at the office just before eleven due to a scheduled meeting outside of the office. The first person I saw was the receptionist.

"Good morning, Marlene," I said pleased to see her, but she just smiled. A month earlier, Helen, was promoted from her secretary title to my administrative assistant. When I got upstairs to my office, Helen told me that Jeff Silver needed to speak with me.

"Thank you. I'd like to talk to you about a rumor going around the office."

"What rumor?" she asked confused.

"I'll speak with you later."

When I entered the general manager's office, Jeff had a concerned look on his face.

"Jeff, what's the matter?" I asked, sitting down.

"We're going to have to get a new receptionist."

"Why? What happened? I just saw Marlene when I came in and she looked happy."

"She might be, but she gave me her two weeks notice this morning."

"What was her reason?"

"She told me that her school's trimester was about to begin and she wants to finish her B.S. degree program during the day."

"Wow, I had no idea. I'll get Helen on this right away."

"I already told Helen to place an ad in the papers," Jeff said.

"I'm going to speak with Marlene, if you don't mind. She just told me last week how much she enjoyed working here."

"That's fine, but I think she's pretty set about leaving."

I left Jeff's office and asked Helen to have someone relieve Marlene so I could meet with her.

"I thought you wanted to speak with me about a rumor?" Helen snapped.

"I do, but that can wait." I never got the opportunity to speak with Helen.

When Marlene came into my office, she closed the door behind her. The company had an open door policy, so if it was a closed-door meeting, it must be serious or a private nature and it was necessary to have a witness. We called it the 'Nancy Arnett Rule'.

"You don't have to close the door," I advised.

"I feel more comfortable with it closed."

"Well, okay," I said sounding uncomfortable with my decision.

She appeared nervous and a little disappointed with what she was about to share. I didn't understand why the sudden change in her, yet I needed to understand why.

"Look, I really enjoyed the time we spent together," she said dropping her head. Her long hair covered her beautiful face until she took her hand and brushed it back. "And if there's any truth to the rumor I heard, it would be difficult to have time together on a regular basis if I continued to work here."

"Jeff told me that you're leaving because you want to attend school full-time."

"That's partially true," she admitted, blushing. "But the other reason is because I want to spend more time with you."

Until now, my experience in California brought one shocking disappointment after another, but this seemed to be a good and welcome shock to my system.

"I'm flattered you feel that way and to be honest, I feel the same way." We both smiled and hugged briefly. "Let's just keep the relationship on a business level until you leave. We can plan our first dinner after that."

"That sounds great."

What followed was the longest two weeks I ever experienced. On her final day, the sales staff, a couple of administrative staff members and management took her out for appetizers and drinks after work. It was a nice going away party that she really enjoyed. We all promised that we would stay in touch. I was sure I would be staying in touch more than anyone else at the party.

In our platonic relationship, I found Marlene to be an intelligent, charming, and engaging woman. From what I observed, she was a loving mother and enjoyed sports on all levels. Her beauty was an added bonus. She seemed like the perfect person for me to get to know better. Over the next few weeks, after she left the company, we spoke daily and met for lunch twice before finally having our first date. She made the dinner reservations at a romantic quaint restaurant in Long Beach. Needless to say, we had a wonderful time.

"We have to do this more often," I claimed.

"Okay, but dinner will be on me next time."

"You're on."

I was quite surprised that she actually offered to pay for our next dinner. I must have died and gone to heaven. The tab that night was over three hundred dollars.

Finally, we received word from corporate that the EECO and the California Department of Fair Employment complaints were dismissed. The company and I were absolved of any wrongdoing. I was elated with the great news and I wanted to go out to celebrate the ruling. I called Marlene and asked if she was available to meet me for cocktails that evening and she agreed.

We'd been discreet with our public interaction until that evening. We never met in the evening at any downtown venue. If we were seen by anyone from the office, this would be our coming out party. It wasn't surprising when we ran into Mark Sullivan, our general sales manager, and one of his female account executives. We were at a popular nightspot and a 'meet market' for many media types.

"Hi Marlene, it's been a while. How've you been?" Mark asked with a suggestive grin.

"Wonderful and how are you?"

"Good, thanks." Mark shook my hand and joked, "What? You're not at work?"

"I have to have some fun, don't you think?"

Everyone at the office knew I was a workaholic and the running joke was that I needed to get a life. It was true. I needed more balance in my life. My demanding workload prevented me from making frequent trips back home so I didn't have much interaction with my family. It was my hope that Marlene would help provide that balance. Over a few glasses of wine, I admitted that the rumor she heard about me and the company was true. However, we'd just been informed that the case had been resolved and all charges were dismissed.

"That's great news. You do have a reason to celebrate. As a matter of fact, I was planning to invite you to my home for dinner. We can continue the celebration there."

"I would love to have a home cooked meal. It's been a long time."

As we were leaving the restaurant, she handed me a paper and said, "Here's my address. I'll see you Saturday evening at seven."

"Have a good night," I told her before kissing her gently on the cheek.

My week was busy and seemed to go by rather fast. I was looking forward to our dinner. That Saturday, I arrived right on time. I brought a bottle of merlot, her favorite wine, and handed it to her when she answered the door. As I slipped off my shoes, I admired the artwork hanging on her wall. It was a painting of white flowers with a hint of pink on the tip of the pedals. They were delicate and captivating.

Marlene followed my gaze to the painting and stated, "They're Colchicum flowers; my absolute favorite. Follow me." She led me into the living room and I took a seat on the sofa as she continued to the kitchen.

She called out, "Dinner is almost ready. Would you like a glass of wine before dinner?"

"That would be fine."

"I have a bottle of Dom Perignon for our celebration after dinner."

"I'm impressed. Where's Billy and your daughter, Sarah?" I asked glancing around. "I thought I'd be able to meet her."

"It's their father's weekend."

She didn't show any worry about the fact that we were alone in her home without her children. Normally this wouldn't be an issue, but I had an uneasy feeling about it. I guess I was still a little paranoid about the whole Nancy Arnett affair.

Her culinary skills were impressive as dinner was delicious and the wine managed to put me at ease. She prepared my favorite dessert, Tiramisu, and rented *Sleepless in Seattle*, which I hadn't seen. During the movie, we had champagne and popcorn. I was extremely full and a little tipsy by the end of the night.

"I should be headed back to town, it's getting late," I said, sounding a bit tired.

"James, you've had a lot to drink, are you okay to drive?" Before I could answer she added, "I have a guest room, so you're welcome to stay."

"Oh, I'm okay. I'll just call a taxi and get my car tomorrow. Can I use your phone?"

"Sure," she said, pointing in its direction.

"Anyways, my kids always call me early Sunday morning."

After I made the call and hung up, I returned to the couch. Unexpectedly, Marlene leaned over and gave me a hug coupled with a passionate kiss.

"That was a nice surprise."

"Yes, and our first real kiss," she added sweetly.

Marlene and I talked for a while longer before I saw headlights flash in the front window and then a horn blew a couple of notes. As I got up and walked towards the door, we hugged again and with a disappointed look on her face, she said, "Good night."

I think she really wanted me to stay and I'm sure this was one of the few times, in her adult life, that she didn't get her way. I believe that was the night she determined that would never happen again.

The next day, I called to thank her for a wonderful time and told her I'd stop by to pick up my car. I asked if her children were back home and she indicated that they were on their way. We never really spoke about her ex-husband. Based on her lifestyle, beautiful home, and the fact that his home was located in the Hollywood Hills, he must have been wealthy. I remember when I finally met him; I was surprised by his appearance. He was a short middle-aged man with a receding hairline, wearing jeans and cowboy boots. I didn't view him as having been Marlene's type.

"Marlene, what does your ex do for a living?"

She hesitated before stating, "He's a businessman and real estate investor."

"He must be good at what he does from what I can see."

"You can say that. He really loves our daughter."

"What about your son," I asked with growing curiosity.

"It's a long story. I can't talk about it right now," she said dismissively. "I hear the kids coming in. I have to go but I'll call you later."

She hung up the phone before I could say goodbye. I was hit with yet another strange feeling and decided I needed to do some research on Marlene's ex-husband. I didn't have a good night sleep, as I felt something was bothering Marlene and I had to get to the bottom of it.

Work was going well. We upgraded the staff, which alleviated the pressure for me to be so hands-on. I delegated some of my duties so I'd have more time to develop better systems regarding the reports required by corporate. In addition, I had more time to network with other advertising agency executives. I began going to business meetings with the general manager, as well as the sales manager. During a recent trip to a meeting with Mark Sullivan, he asked about Marlene and me.

"I was surprised to see you guys together at Brio's."

"After she left the company, we started hanging out."

Mark shook his head and said, "Lucky you."

"Yeah, I know."

If only I really knew. While I had the opportunity, I started searching for information on Marlene's ex-husband.

I ordered a background check on Mr. Allen, at my own expense, to see what he really did for a living. I was interested in discovering what type of business he was involved in because I wondered if all his dealings and investments were legitimate. He was the owner of an upscale auto repair shop and he owned several apartment buildings. Something came up that I wanted to explore further, but I thought Marlene might be able to shed light on the subject. The background check indicated that the original owner of the repair shop was a woman named Denise Johnson-Allen. I assumed she was related to Marlene's ex-husband. I decided to ask her about the woman. I had to be tactful, but kept in mind that it could be a sensitive topic. Marlene typically called me at the close of business each day to see how my day had gone. When she called, I reminded her that she said she would talk with me regarding her comment about her ex-husband who loved his daughter, but didn't have the same feelings for his son.

"I remember the conversation and you deserve an explanation." After a beat, she added, "When will you have time to talk?"

"How about tomorrow night? You know where I live, so let's meet at my apartment."

"Wow, your apartment? I must be special," she joked, lightening the mood.

Thus far, I had never invited her to my place. The only person who had seen my apartment was J.R.

"You're special. And to prove my point, I'll order Chinese for dinner." I knew she loved Chinese food.

While I was taking down plates for the food, I heard a faint knock on the door. I casually walked over, unlocked the door, and opened it. As always, she looked great.

"What a nice apartment! Did you furnish it yourself?"

"No, but spending two thousand two hundred dollars a month for a one bedroom apartment better be nicely furnished."

"You're right about that," she laughed.

As we started eating, she switched to a more serious conversation. She revealed that Billy wasn't her ex-husband's actual son; he was her nephew who they adopted when he was three years old. Billy was one of her older sisters' children, but she wanted to give him up for adoption because she was a Las Vegas Showgirl. She felt it wouldn't be a good environment to raise a child. She admitted that her ex-husband always resented her sister for not taking care of her responsibilities. At times, his feelings were transferred to Billy.

"I feel bad about the situation and it was one of the reasons I divorced him."

"Billy is such a great kid. I can't see how anyone couldn't love him, but why did Billy spend last weekend with him?"

"Billy's little sister loves him dearly and won't visit her father without him."

"Wow, that's unbelievable."

I decided to introduce my questions about Lawrence Allen and Denise Allen.

"Marlene, you should know by now I really care about you. Leaving you last Saturday was difficult for me, but I just felt it was still too early in our relationship for me to sleep over."

She laughed and said, "That made me care for you more."

"Really? I thought you would feel I was a coward."

She laughed again and replied, "That thought crossed my mind."

My smile grew wider. I had several questions so I opened up the conversation. "Who's Denise Allen?"

Marlene's entire expression changed. She looked like she had seen a ghost. "Why are you asking about Denise?"

"Like I said, I really care about you and I want to be in a serious relationship. Clearly, that'll involve your children so I think we need to be honest with one another about our history. Since their father is actively involved, I want to be sure a long-term relationship is possible."

"James," she huffed, "Lawrence is a control freak and in the past, he's interfered in my personal business. He does it by withholding child support, so I have to take him to court. It's inconvenient, but I have to do what I have to do!"

"I understand that, but you haven't answered the question. Who is Denise? Is she one of his relatives?"

I was taken aback by Marlene's cold emotional response.

"She's his ex-wife and she's dead!" She noticed I'd grown uncomfortable so she smiled and recoiled by trying to rephrase her response. "I'm sorry she died, but I just didn't like that woman."

"You knew her? How did she die?"

"She was killed in a horrific car crash. James, this is a difficult subject for me and I'd prefer not to discuss it. Let's talk about something else, laugh, and have fun like we always do. That's why I love spending time with you. You make me happy and give me a chance to forget about my problems."

"Okay then, let's change the subject."

She generated even more questions about her showgirl, deadbeat sister and Lawrence's deceased ex-wife. Marlene left my apartment around ten that evening after a long embrace and kiss good night.

I was conflicted again. My feelings for Marlene were growing stronger each day, but there was something mysterious about her past that I needed to know. Lawrence Allen's auto shop was a successful business that was frequented by many of the professional athletes and celebrities in the L.A. area. My sales manager had a friend, Charlie Wells, who knew Lawrence well so I asked Mark if he'd introduce me. One evening, Mark was meeting his friend after work and said I could come. However, Mark couldn't stay long because he had another appointment. We met Charlie at a small restaurant in West Hollywood. Charlie was a former professional athlete who knew both of Lawrence's former wives Denise and Marlene. After one drink, Mark left and I had Charlie one on one. Charlie was the type of person who wanted people to know how much he knew and he certainly knew a lot about Lawrence Allen. After a few drinks, he was on a roll. I didn't have to ask questions because he was giving me more information than I needed, but still, I listened attentively. I learned quite a bit.

Denise Johnson-Allen was the money behind Lawrence's wealth while she was alive and well after her death. She was ten years older than Lawrence and discovered him at a small auto repair shop. She felt he was a gifted mechanic and they could make big money by opening an auto repair shop in downtown L.A. that catered to a high-end clientele. The concept worked and after five years of building a successful business, she decided they should get married.

Ten years into their thriving partnership, a beautiful young woman drove a vintage BMW into the shop. He asked this 19-year-old her name and where she acquired her fine vehicle. She told him her name was Marlene and it was her father's car. Her father was a pastor at a local AME church. She told Lawrence her father let her drive the car, but lately, it was giving her problems. Lawrence gave her a loaner car to use while her car was being repaired. Although it was unusual for such a young customer to be given this type of service, Lawrence was smitten.

Over the next twelve months, Marlene returned several times to get her car serviced and to talk with Lawrence while she waited for the minor service. During these visits, Lawrence noticed the attention she garnered from his clients, the professional athletes in particular. One day, Denise was at the shop and asked Lawrence who the woman was because she was attracting so much attention, including his. She wanted to know why the old BMW was at the shop so often.

About two months later, Denise confronted Lawrence about his relationship with Marlene. As the story goes, they had a violent argument so she left their home and spent the day drinking with a girlfriend. She told her friend she thought Lawrence was having an affair with the young girl who was always at the shop. While heading home to the Hollywood Hills and very intoxicated, she took a curve at a high speed, lost control of the car, and died in the fiery crash.

After an extensive insurance investigation, the accident was due to driving under the influence and not by a mechanical defect as some of Denise's family alleged. Lawrence was the sole beneficiary of Denise's three million dollar policy and the business received a three million dollar award from her Key Person insurance policy.

Lawrence Allen was now a rich man with a financially stable business. He married Marlene Hughes nine months later and she started working at the shop. Lawrence felt she was great for business, especially with his high profile male clientele. He had his trophy wife and wanted her in his sight at all times.

My meeting with Charlie Wells was a revelation. Marlene's ex-husband wasn't a big time drug dealer. For some reason, I thought that might have been the case. Instead, his money came from a large insurance settlement and a successful auto repair business. I was pleased to know his money came from a legit source or that would have told me something else about Marlene. However, the death of the first wife and his marriage to Marlene in less than a year was a little disconcerting. The fact that Denise's family thought that foul play was the cause of her accident

.ıas scary. I decided not to discuss my findings with Marlene, but the information was filed in the back of my mind.

The following weekend, Marlene and I were scheduled for another session of racquetball. We'd played a few times since our first game and I was getting better. In fact, that day, I won two out of the three games. Marlene was competitive, but I was surprised with her reaction to the first time she lost to me. She hit the last ball wildly against the wall when I scored the games winning point, then she banged her racket on the floor.

"You really don't like losing."

"I hate losing, and losing to a beginner really makes me mad."

"Even me?"

"Yes, even you!" she said raising her voice.

I thought to myself, her reaction was over the top and maybe we shouldn't play anymore. After what seemed like a long minute of silence, she grabbed her faculties, realizing her actions were extreme.

She looked at me with her striking emerald eyes and stated, "You're improving. I must be a good teacher."

I could tell she was still seething.

"You are. But I'm bigger, stronger, and faster than you. I had to start winning a few right?" She didn't answer, so I hastily changed the topic. "Let's grab something to eat."

"I'm famished, but after lunch do you mind if we go to your apartment and talk?"

"Of course we can. What's on your mind?"

"Nothing important, I just want to talk in a quiet space and your place is perfect. Besides, I love your view."

The view from my apartment was great when the smog didn't ruin it. My apartment was located in a luxury high-rise building on the thirtieth floor. When we entered the apartment, her focus was drawn to the view.

"It's such a nice day. Let's sit out on the terrace."

"I'll get us something to drink and I'll meet you outside."

For the next two hours, we sat on my terrace and I listened. Occasionally, I had questions. I asked Marlene to give me a detailed description of her family and the environment in which she was raised. She told me, a few weeks prior, her mother mentioned she wanted to meet the man who had captured so much of her time. She explained that she was extremely close to her mother and shared a lot with her. She described her mother as a spiritual person who had been married to two pastors in her life. Her first husband was thirty years her senior and he passed away after twelve years of marriage. She said he was the father of her two older sisters and brother. Her dad was the former pastor at a large AME church in L.A. and was her mother's second husband. He was the father of Marlene's two other sisters.

"So when am I going to meet your mom and family?"

"Soon. Very soon."

She continued, by telling me that she didn't have a happy childhood. Her older siblings were jealous of her because of the special attention she received from her mom and especially her dad. They taunted, teased, and verbally abused her on a daily basis. She felt they would've physically harmed her if she complained to her parents. Marlene claimed it contributed to why Billy's mother got pregnant and left town when she was seventeen. I assumed she was being mistreated as well.

"How is your relationship with your brother and sisters now?"

"I have a good relationship with my brother, but I just tolerate my sisters out of respect for my mother."

I got the impression she liked her brother but his older sisters negatively influenced him when he was young.

"I don't think I want to meet your sisters."

"You probably won't."

She pulled a family photo out of her purse. As I studied the picture, I noticed Marlene didn't look anything like her siblings, and from my count, one sister wasn't in the photo.

"One sister is missing from the picture. And I'm sorry, but you don't look like anyone in this picture."

"Billy's mom is missing. She's my complexion and we have similar hair. When you meet my parents, you'll see that I have features from both."

"I look forward to meeting them."

She looked out over the city and took a sip of wine while appearing to be putting her thoughts in chronological order.

"I met Lawrence a year after I graduated from high school at his auto repair shop. He was really nice to me and never charged me for repairs. I was driving my dad's old car and it was having mechanical issues. He asked me to come by to meet some of his famous customers and I thought he was just trying to impress me. Sometimes he gave me gifts."

"I guess he liked you," I said sarcastically but she ignored my comment and continued.

"A couple of times, his wife saw me there. Her office was located in a downtown office building, so she was rarely at the shop. I was introduced to her once by one of Lawrence's clients and she wasn't very nice."

"Why? What did she do?"

"Well, when I reached out to shake her hand she just said a curt, 'Hello' and then she turned and walked away. The customer and I just looked at each other in disbelief."

"That must have been embarrassing."

"I thought so," she said shrugging. "Later that day, I called Lawrence to ask him what was wrong with his wife."

"What did he say?"

"Nothing, other than she's just a bitch. Several months after that I got a call from Lawrence telling me that his wife was just killed in a car crash."

"How did you respond to the news?"

"Oh well, I told him I was sorry and asked if I could do anything for him. About a year later, we got married."

"Wow!"

"I know. I've laid a lot of information on you, so what do you think?"

"Apparently you've had your share of challenges. I'm happy you survived your childhood and although we haven't discussed much, a difficult marriage to Lawrence."

"True, but we'll save that discussion for another day."

We got up, went inside and spent the rest of the day watching NCAA football. I still had questions about Marlene circulating in my head, though it wasn't the time to force the topics. Intuitively, something was nagging at me but I wanted to let it go. After Marlene left my place, I reflected on the conversation. I felt she was honest about the situation with Lawrence and it confirmed my research and conversation with Charlie a couple weeks ago. Her family sounded a little dysfunctional and I'm sure it had an affect on her. However, most people who looked at her family picture would have thought she was adopted. I know I did. Marlene called to say good night and let me know she was taking me to meet her mother that upcoming weekend. I couldn't wait.

I received a surprising call that week at the office. It was Kamiah Terry, our former receptionist who went to lunch and never returned.

I answered, "This is Fairchild, how can I help you?"

"Hello Mr. Fairchild, this is Kamiah Terry. Do you remember me?"

"Absolutely," I replied. "You're our receptionist who went AWOL, we put an APB out on you," I joked.

She laughed and said, "I'm sorry. I wanted to apologize for handling my situation so poorly."

"It's my understanding that the promoter made you a great offer but you're right, you didn't handle it professionally. Kamiah, always remember, as you go forward in your career, communication is the key. If you returned from lunch and asked to meet with me to discuss your new opportunity, I would've understood that time was of the essence for you. We would have been supportive."

"I'm sorry. You're right."

"By the way, we've had two new receptionists since you left, so it's an important but transitional position in any organization. If you were good at the job, you would have been able to move up here, or elsewhere."

"I didn't think of that."

"So how's your new job?"

"It's wonderful! I work for one of the largest entertainment and event companies in the country. And that's the other reason I'm calling. I have access to tickets to the best concerts, plays, and sporting events. I'd like to give you front row tickets to the Frankie Beverly and Maze concert coming to L.A. at the end of the month."

"Wow, that's great! I love them and I haven't attended a concert since I've been here."

"If you need tickets to any event across the country, I'm only a phone call away."

"Thank you, Kamiah."

"I hear things are going well at Ascending Media Group and I know you have a lot to do with the success. You were always nice to me."

"Thank you, but it's a team effort. I wish you continued success and I'll keep in touch." Since I was developing a social life with Marlene, this created other options other than going out to restaurants and playing racquetball. My life was starting to pickup, but I really missed my kids and I needed to schedule a trip back home soon.

I got married right after I graduated from college with my bachelor's degree in accounting. I met my wife in college, but she dropped out after her sophomore year. She felt she needed a job to help her family financially. She was a great student and we used to work together on school projects. I felt bad for her when she decided to quit. We remained close and started dating seriously during my junior year. We got engaged my senior year and married in August after my graduation. We were great friends, but in hindsight, we were too young and in my case, too immature for marriage. She was close to her family, so anytime something came up with them, she felt obligated to return home to help. Once our daughter was born a year later, I became third in line. The things we argued about were trivial, but at the time, I thought they were so significant. Money was always the biggest issue.

Our son was born four years later. He wasn't planned, but I was happy to have a son. After seven years of an unhappy marriage, we decided to separate and I filed for a divorce. We were much better friends than lovers and remained friends. She was a great mother and raised our two wonderful children, who I missed dearly. I felt I needed to go to graduate school to help accelerate my career. I decided a MBA program would be completed in less time because of my undergraduate degree in business. I applied to three of the best 'B' schools in New England and attended the school that awarded me the most grant money.

It was the weekend and I was on my way to pick up Marlene for the drive to her mother's house. Her parent's lived in a nice middle class area on the West Side of Los Angeles. Marlene lived in Brentwood, which was a twenty-minute drive.

"Are you excited to meet my family? Everyone's going to be there."

"Even your older sisters?"

"Yes. Everyone wants to meet you."

"Wow, I want to meet him too," I joked.

"You're so silly," she replied. When we arrived, I began to get nervous. As we walked up the driveway, she grabbed my hand and said, "It's going to be alright. They're going to like you."

It was a full house; everyone was there, including her teenage niece. The only one missing was Billy's mother. I shook everyone's hand and hugged Marlene's parents. The family looked pretty much like the photo, but I must admit the older sisters were more attractive in person. Her mother prepared an extensive brunch and the food was excellent. We talked about my background, parents, children, religion, and plans for the future. I felt like I was back on the witness stand. Marlene was protective, so when a question became too personal, she intervened. Her father seemed to enjoy observing the interaction, but he was the one who asked about my church affiliation and religion. I guess my biggest surprise was how nice the older sisters were and the daughter of the eldest sister. I envisioned Marlene's childhood growing up with the evil sisters in the Cinderella story. Marlene was waiting to be rescued by Prince Charming. I guess time heals all wounds. I had a wonderful time and hugged everyone before leaving.

On the drive home, I declared, "I like your family. I'm surprised how nice your older sisters were."

"They're great actresses. They should be in the movies."

There was coldness in her tone that never surfaced during our two-hour visit with her family. At times, I thought Marlene was a pretty good actress herself.

"After meeting your parents, it's obvious that you have your mother's eyes and nose. You have your father's hair."

"Yeah right!"

Releasing soft laughter, she punched me on my arm. Her father was bald. When we arrived at her house, I got out of the car and walked her to her door.

"Marlene, I have front row seats to the Frankie Beverly and Maze concert in two weeks, but isn't that your weekend to have the kids?"

"I love Frankie Beverly and Maze. I'll just tell Lawrence to keep Sarah and Billy that weekend. It won't be a problem. That would be exciting!"

"I think so too, but listen, I can't come in. I have a report to complete for Monday's sales meeting."

"That's fine. Just call me when you get home."

"I will. And I had a good time meeting your family." She gave me a quick kiss and closed the door.

There were several red flags I should have noticed. Maybe I did, but obviously I chose to ignore them. Her beauty and my desire to be in the relationship blinded me. Marlene always made me feel like I was her top priority. When you want something, but ignore your intuition, sometimes there's a price to pay.

Chapter 3

The Lure & the Passion

The Frankie Beverly and Maze concert was on Friday at the downtown music center. Since it was a three-day weekend, I called Marlene and told her I made plans for us after the concert.

"What plans?" she questioned, sounding excited.

"I made reservations for this weekend at a beach resort in Malibu."

"That sounds amazing."

When I hung up the phone, I had the feeling that I'd made her day and hopefully her weekend.

The day flew by and I found myself driving to Marlene's house for the start of a fun weekend. She opened her door and my mouth dropped open. She was dressed in a form-fitting black leather pantsuit like Halle Berry wore in *Cat Woman*. I'd never seen her dress so sensually. She was always conservative at work and when we were on dates. She wore form-fitting outfits at the gym when we played racquetball so I knew she had a great body, but this was different for her.

She saw my expression and asked, "Is something wrong? You don't like my suit?"

"No, that's not it, you look stunning. I just have to go get a pistol to keep people from staring," I replied.

"Come on silly, let's get to the concert, I don't want to be late."

On the way to the concert, she told me how happy she was about our surprise weekend. She reminded me that this would be the first time we would be staying together. Marlene was making fun of me for the time I didn't spend the night at her house. I recalled how Marlene would enter a room and all heads turned in her direction. However, I was living that experience from another perspective. She had universal appeal as we made our way to the front row seats. I felt like Kevin Costner in *The Bodyguard*. Los Angeles was full of beautiful people, so I was quite surprised at the reaction she was getting. On one of our dinner dates, an older Caucasian woman approached us to tell Marlene that she was a handsome woman. I'd never heard that word used to describe a woman, but she meant it as a compliment.

Frankie Beverly put on a great show. Marlene enjoyed the concert and all the attention she was receiving. I imagined men were jealous and wondering why she was with me, but I've been told that I'm a good-looking guy. My ex-wife and other friends in my life were attractive as well. I'm 6'2", well-groomed, and in good shape. Many people like my GQ style of dress and I was looking pretty good at the concert. I saw some women taking a quick peek. However, I wasn't stopping traffic like Marlene.

On our thirty-minute drive to Malibu, she explained that she had many provocative outfits, but her ex-husband would never let her wear them. She added that they never went to concerts or the theater. He was a real homebody, but he did like hunting, fishing, and horseback riding, which she enjoyed too.

I concluded that she lived a sheltered life. After growing up in a religious home and then being married to an older, settled man, I believed she was looking for some excitement. I was planning to provide some excitement that weekend. The resort had access to a private beach, all oceanfront rooms and exotic massages, so there were plenty stimuli to get her in the mood. It was about midnight when we reached the resort.

Although we were beginning to become intimate, she abruptly stopped and said, "I have a surprise for you tomorrow, so let's get some sleep." We quickly fell asleep in each other's arms.

The next morning, after freshening up, we jumped back in bed to start where we left off the night before. There was no stopping this time. Marlene was assertive in bed; she knew what she liked and she let me know. As she was getting more excited, I was already there; she slipped underneath the blue sheet and said, "Oh my, this was worth the wait." The pressure was on. I was twenty years old the first time I had sex, however, I did read about sex and how to please a woman years before that experience. I knew to spend plenty of time on foreplay. What I hadn't experienced was a woman who knew a man's erogenous zones. Marlene used my ears, the back of my knees, inner thighs, the nape of my neck, and feet to take me to a place I'd never been. She whispered softly into my ear, "I love being your naked lady." Our explosive lovemaking included simultaneous and multiple orgasms all weekend long. Her big surprise was introducing me to her sex toy, which she used to have more intense orgasms. She didn't have to use it often once we were together. You would never imagine, based on Marlene's outward calm demeanor, that she had a little freak in her and I loved it. The resort had some great features, however, Sunday evening was the only time we came up for air. After a romantic candlelight dinner, we took a casual walk on the private beach. Needless to say, it was a spectacular weekend and we were both hooked on one another.

The word *love* was used many times that weekend and one of the positive things Marlene did for me was to appreciate the true meaning of love. She wasn't afraid of it. Obviously, at that stage of our relationship, we had strong feelings for each other. I didn't realize until later that those feelings were masked by heavy infatuation, not true love.

During our drive home, we talked about how we were so much alike. Meaning, our outward appearance and actions disguised the fiery intensity we had inside. The conversation turned serious when I told her that I had strong feelings for her and wanted to take her back East to meet my parents.

"My mother lives in Boston and my dad is in D.C. We can fly to Boston, rent a car and drive to New York City, spend a couple of days there and head to D.C."

"That sounds like a lot of driving. Is it?"

"No, not really. Boston is four hours from N.Y. and N.Y. to D.C. is about four hours. It's a straight shot. I'll take 95 south all the way."

"I suppose I could have Lawrence and my mother handle the kids."

"What about your classes? Can you miss ten days of school?"

"That's not a problem," she replied.

We didn't talk about school much, but I figured she knew what she was doing. We decided to make the trip a month later. That gave her enough time to make arrangements for her children and I could forewarn my parents. In addition, I could let J.R. know that I'd be in D.C. for a couple of days and stop by the office.

During that month, I didn't see Marlene too much. We made love once, which was at her house when the kids were with their father. It was similar to the first time, although I think I was still recovering from our wild weekend in Malibu. I finally met her daughter, Sarah, that same weekend when she returned home. She was a pretty little girl, polite, and respectful. She enjoyed sports like, Billy, but for some reason, her parents didn't let her play any organized sports.

My parents divorced when my brother and I were still in elementary school. Just like my first wife, they were much better friends than husband and wife. My dad was pretty mild mannered and got along with everyone. My mother, Alma, was a loving woman but a taskmaster. Anything we did, we had to do well regardless if it was school, church, chores, or anything else. She was extremely protective and if anyone bothered her kids, they had to deal with her. My mother lived with my Aunt Vera, her younger sister, who was a consultant for the state government. We grew up in the projects until I was twelve but we never wanted for anything. I didn't realize how poor we were until I went to college and someone didn't believe I was raised in The Old Colony Housing Projects. My mother was now far removed from the projects and lived in a luxury apartment building overlooking the Boston Commons.

Marlene was both excited and nervous about meeting my parents. I assured her, they were nice and she'd like them. I was certain they would definitely like her. I didn't tell her how my mother reacted when I said I wanted to marry my first wife, Linda, because I liked to have fun. I knew that I was the cause of her unrestrained tirade. She responded furiously at my ignorance in thinking marriage was going to be fun. She set me straight, letting me know it wasn't about fun in a way I didn't think I'd ever forget. I was rather naïve back then and she was absolutely right. At that point, Marlene and I never spoke about getting married so that wouldn't be an issue.

We landed at Logan Airport at noon eastern time. I told my mom we didn't need to be picked up because I'd rent a car. Marlene packed three suitcases and one carry-on for the visit, so I was looking forward to seeing the outfits she never had a chance to wear. I rented a full-sized car that would have enough trunk space for our luggage since I had two suitcases. During the flight, I learned that she never met Lawrence's parents who were elderly and living in Texas. In addition, this would be her first East Coast visit; she was interested in seeing a Broadway play, and of course, the garment district.

We arrived at Mom's apartment and we were greeted with an abundance of hugs and kisses. My mother was affectionate; no one was treated like a stranger.

"Jimmy, she's beautiful. How did you get her?"

I let out a hardy chuckle and shrugged my shoulders. Even my mother asked the same question everyone was thinking. Only family and friends who grew up with me called me Jimmy and I'm sure her comments made Marlene's day.

"Are you guys hungry? I ordered your favorite Indian food, Jimmy." By the look on Marlene's face, I could tell Indian cuisine would be a new experience for her.

She replied, "Indian food? She's Indian?"

I said, "No and it's like Chinese food, only better."

My Aunt Vera wasn't as warm and cuddly to Marlene. She had a funny look on her face when she heard Marlene's comment about the Indian food. Lunch was excellent and Marlene seemed to genuinely enjoy it. We were tired from the long flight and decided to take a quick nap after lunch. We played around a little before dozing off in each other's arms.

That evening, we separated so Marlene could spend time with my mother. That gave Aunt Vera a chance to give me the third degree. She didn't hesitate to speak her mind.

"She really didn't know the food was from India?"

"Maybe not. She's led a sheltered life and hasn't been exposed to many things outside of California."

Vera responded sarcastically by asking, "They don't have Indian food in L.A.?"

"Stop. She likes Chinese food."

"James, I know you just met her, but I don't get a good vibe from her. You know, that L.A. plastic phony thing."

Slightly annoyed I said, "Marlene's an intelligent, loving person, and a great mother. She'll be getting her college degree in a few months." I love my Aunt and I knew she was only looking out for my best interest, but I continued. "Listen Vera, why don't you spend some time with Marlene. I'm sure once you get to know her, you might like her."

"That's a good idea. We'll get together tomorrow."

After breakfast, Vera stated she had some errands to run and invited Marlene to go with her. Marlene seemed hesitant.

"Oh, Marlene, it'll be fun. You've never been to Boston, so I'll show you the sites. We'll do some shopping and have a nice lunch."

"Vera knows this city like the back of her hand. I'm sure you'll enjoy yourself," my mother added with a sincere lighthearted tone.

Marlene responded, "Well, Mom, if you and James don't mind, I'm sure it'll be fun."

"I'll be ready to go by ten," Vera told her.

I spent the next six hours with my mother. We talked about Marlene, who she thought was a fine young lady. I explained the craziness at work was finally over and I was adjusting to the California lifestyle.

"You look happy so something is definitely agreeing with you."

"I suppose you're right," I replied reaching over for a hug.

Marlene and my aunt returned a little after four that afternoon. Marlene was carrying two large shopping bags and I asked, "So you found something you like?"

"Yeah," she said in a short huff, brushing past me as she continued to the guest bedroom. It was easy to detect that something was bothering her. I turned to Vera for answers.

"Vera, is everything alright?"

"I'm fine, but you should speak to your girlfriend," she said pointing towards the guest bedroom.

I went into the bedroom and asked Marlene, "Are you okay?"

"What did you tell your aunt about me?"

"Nothing much. I said you're a great mother, smart, and about to graduate from college. Why?"

We started the day off well and saw famous landmarks, shopped at a nice boutique, and then went to lunch around two o'clock. That's when Vera started interrogating me about my children, their father, and my plans after I graduate!"

"Okay. That doesn't sound like an interrogation. She just wanted to get know you better."

With an unforeseen fury, she turned to face me and snapped, "I'm a private person! She was just being nosey! Don't ever tell anyone my business again!"

My mouth fell open because I was shocked. I didn't know where her defensiveness was coming from, but it came with ferocity. I couldn't fathom why she was like that.

"You're upset. I'll leave you alone until you calm down."

I left the room to speak with Vera and find out about what went wrong. My mother was lying down in her room so I was able to talk to Vera alone. Vera was a successful business consultant who specialized in market analysis and contract negotiations. She was great at asking the right questions to get the information she needed. Vera's first words out of her mouth were, "Watch yourself!"

Still stunned about everything that was taking place, I replied, "Why? What are you talking about?"

"I'll tell you this much. The day was fine until lunch. When I began asking questions, her mood changed dramatically. Marlene got very defensive when I asked about her ex-husband and her future plans. Jimmy, I know I can be hardcore, so my questions were straightforward but courteous. I don't trust Marlene. She reminds me of an attractive woman I knew in the past and she was a gold digger.

I interjected, "Vera, now you know I'm not rich."

"But does she know that?"

Vera continued telling me about the old friend that would seek out vulnerable, gullible men and use her charm and beauty to get what she wanted. Then she would dump them. She was totally heartless and had no remorse for her victims. Finally, Vera told me she loved me and didn't want me to get hurt. She hoped her instincts were wrong.

"Thank you for your concern, Vera. You're probably wrong about Marlene, but I'll keep my eyes open."

"At the very least do that. Keep a watch on that woman."

When Marlene came out of the bedroom, her mood had changed completely. She said she just spoke to her kids. Their father took them to Disneyland for the day as a surprise. She approached Vera to apologize for her attitude and blamed it on never being that far away from her children. Vera told her that she understood and there was no need to apologize. The remainder of the visit went well, although she didn't have much interaction with my aunt after that. We were on our way to New York after a three-day visit. My mother liked her a lot but my aunt still wanted me to watch myself. I could see Vera's point.

During the four-hour drive to New York, we discussed the visit. She really liked my mom and didn't like Aunt Vera. She felt she was too cold and serious. I explained Vera was my mother's youngest sister who came to live with us after graduating from high school. She's seven years older than me, but as I grew older, she became more of a big sister to me. I always called her for advice, especially in regards to business, and she was being protective of me.

"More protective than your mother?"

"I didn't say that. My mother would be ready to fight if anyone bothered her boys."

She smiled and said, "I understand that. Listen, I have something to tell you," she began.

"What's on your mind?"

What followed was the first of many bombshells dropped on me during our relationship. "This is something I've wanted to tell you for long time."

"Okay, go on."

"I'm not graduating from college anytime soon because I dropped out of school months ago."

"Why didn't you tell me this before?"

"I was embarrassed and I didn't want to disappoint you."

"Why should you be? It's not about me. Your education is about you. Why'd you withdraw?"

"The business classes I took were boring and I wasn't doing well. Before I decided to go to college, I worked as a private duty nurse and I found that rewarding. I want to go back to nursing."

I quickly recalled the résumé she presented when she interviewed for the receptionist job and it didn't reflect nursing. On the other hand, Marlene was a nurturing person so working in the field of nursing meant that she enjoyed helping people and working with the sick and elderly.

"Don't be afraid of my reaction to anything you share with me. In business, I tell my staff that I don't like any surprises and that goes double in my personal life."

The conversation that followed was light and involved things we would do in New York City. During my idle time, I thought about my aunt's warning and here we were. Marlene was full of surprises. The reason I was conflicted was because some were good surprises while many were unfavorable. Honesty was important to me, so I would take note of her warning.

Marlene's confession about her college status did wonders for her demeanor. We laughed and joked the remainder of the journey to New York. The three-day stay in the city was a whirlwind. We had dinner at Tavern on the Green and she treated. We saw *Lion King* on Broadway and were even able to get tickets to see the Yankees play the Red Sox. The icing on the cake was making love at the end of the night. She was a completely different person than she was in Boston. I attributed her attitude change to her confession about college and getting away from my Aunt Vera, who truly intimidated her.

We were only in D.C. for two days. The first day we spent time with my dad, where Marlene's charm and affectionate nature was in full effect. My father loved her and she made him feel like he was the best looking older man she'd ever seen. She told him that she knows where his son got his good looks but both of us knew that I looked more like my mother. Dad smiled and appreciated the compliment anyway. While Marlene and Dad were talked, I was able to get away for a few hours to visit my children. The fact I hadn't been able to come home more often was a sore point for their mother and a disappointment for my kids. My short stay did little to correct the situation. My daughter, Lauren, and my son, Daniel, were happy to see me in person as opposed to our weekly phone calls. They are great children and my ex-wife was doing a wonderful job raising them without me, the absentee father. It takes more to being a father than sending monthly child support payments and phone calls. In any event, we had a nice time together and I promised that I would send for them to spend some time with me that summer in California. They seemed pleased as they gave me big hugs and kissed me goodbye. The next day, I took Marlene by our corporate office and she was a big hit there as well. J.R. pulled me aside for a brief meeting, the visit was unofficial so I didn't expect to talk business, but J.R. told me the company was working on a project that would affect the West Coast operations, so he wanted to give me a heads up. Mr. Thompson greeted me like I was a returning hero from a war as he complimented me on the impressive turnaround at Ascending Media Group West.

"We've put an excellent team together and the new general manager and sales manager are doing an outstanding job bringing in new business."

He replied, "Well you are a big part of our success as well."

I thanked him and introduced him to Marlene. Marlene's demeanor at the office was professional and she was dressed in a "Hilary Clinton Style" pantsuit. The president complimented her on her appearance.

"You have a good man here," he told her.

"Yes, I know," she replied.

I diminished the situation in Boston to a slight wobble after that. Marlene was very impressive and I felt she passed the test of meeting my parents and corporate personnel with flying colors. We were on our way to L.A. the next morning.

The Allure of a Predator

Chapter 4

Let's Get Serious

The project that J.R. mentioned to me during my visit to our corporate office involved the acquisition of a small advertising agency. It would serve as a satellite to our L.A. operation. J.R. called to let me know he would be flying to San Francisco the following Tuesday and wanted to meet with me. He sent some documents I needed to review and found the opportunity quite interesting. My daily activities in L.A. were greatly diminished since we upgraded the staff and we had professionals with valuable experience. Being involved in the advertising and sales activities would enhance my career and chances to move into general management at an advertising agency. They were the areas where big salaries and bonuses were paid. It was evident given the outstanding compensation package our new general manager received.

That evening, I met Marlene for drinks. When I told her about my San Francisco opportunity, she was more excited than I was.

"That means we can spend time in the Bay Area?"

"Yeah, it does. I'll probably have to be there two weeks a month," I stated while studying her expression.

"That's wonderful! I love San Francisco and the Napa Valley wine country."

"Out of curiosity, when are you returning to private duty nursing? Are you an RN?"

"No, I'm a licensed practical nurse or LPN. RN's are at a higher level than I am. They can administer medicines, assist physicians in examinations, and they make more money.

"So why didn't you become a registered nurse?"

"The kids were young and Lawrence didn't want me committing so much time to school. A registered nurse requires a four-year program with a Bachelor of Science degree. I got my practical nurse license after finishing a one-year program and passing a test."

"It sounds like Lawrence restricted you from being who you wanted to be in so many ways."

"I told you, he was a control freak."

"I remember you telling me that."

"I'm lining up some potential clients through an employment agency that specializes in nurse placement. I should know something within the next few weeks."

"Once you start working, will you have time to travel with me?"

"I always work with someone who serves as my replacement when I need time off."

"That sounds like a pretty sweet deal."

We kissed good night and I went home to prepare for a staff meeting announcing our new satellite location.

Jeffrey Silver and Mark Sullivan were the only other people who knew about our move to San Francisco. The staff seemed to be excited about the expansion. Expansion meant we were growing our revenue base and allowed the sales staff to generate additional income by adding another major market to sell. After the meeting, Jeffrey asked me to meet in his office.

"This move is a great opportunity for you. I want you to be successful so I'm here for you whenever you need me."

"Thank you. I appreciate that," I said turning to leave.

"Um, there's one more thing, James. While you were on vacation, I received a strange call," he added with his eyebrows arching together.

"What was strange about it?"

"Well, the woman was asking personal questions about you. She asked who you were harassing now."

"What?"

"Yeah. When I asked who was calling she said, 'Sandra Morgan, a good friend of Nancy Arnett. The woman Mr. Fairchild mistreated.'"

"What did you tell her?"

"That I didn't know what she was talking about and I was out of the office."

"I don't know a Sandra Morgan. If she calls again, just transfer the call to me."

"Will do, but it sounds like these women are trying to harass you."

"Could be. Just let me know if she calls again."

I left and headed back to my office. I knew Nancy Arnett wouldn't just go on with her life and appreciate the fact that she's not in jail. Later that afternoon, I called Marlene to tell her about the call and she responded, "Don't worry about it. That situation is behind you now. When are we going to San Francisco? I can't wait." I expected a little more empathy from the woman I hoped to be my soul mate, but it just wasn't there. I ended the call.

It was Tuesday morning and I was on a flight to San Francisco to meet J.R. We leased an office space in the downtown area. I grabbed a cab and headed to the location. When J.R. arrived, we inspected the office space, which was nicely furnished. We wanted to create an attractive environment that projects success and a winning atmosphere. Based upon what I could see, we achieved our goal.

Using Jeff Silver's contacts, we had six potential employees scheduled to interview while we were in town. We planned to hire ten account executives, two administrators and rehire three to four employees from the former company. I would serve as the managing partner, supervising the entire operation. Time management would become critical to my success during this transitional period. While growing skill sets in sales, marketing, and advertising, I had to calculate how much time I needed to complete L.A. and corporate projects. They were still my responsibility. J.R. planned to visit once a month to monitor our progress.

The next few months were both eventful and exciting in regards to my job and relationship with Marlene. We established a schedule where she could spend a weekend with me while I was in San Francisco. She loved the arrangement and so did I. She had a list of activities she wanted us to experience on each visit. Some of the attractions included cycling across the Golden Gate Bridge, dining at the wonderful seafood restaurants, Pier 39 and

Fisherman's Wharf, and walking down Lombard Street, one the world's most crooked streets. Of course we visited the wine country, Muir Woods, and the impressive red wood trees. When I was young, I quit the Boy Scouts because I wasn't an outdoors person, but Marlene's passion for nature and the scenic beauty of Northern California was alluring and eventually claimed me too. We enjoyed the nightlife and concert scene as well. My former receptionist gave us tickets to see Earth, Wind and Fire, Anita Baker, and Luther Vandross perform. Marlene was having the time of her life and I was along for the ride. When I returned to L.A., we did family-oriented activities with Sarah and Billy.

Our relationship had grown stronger and more serious. One evening, we were out having dinner and I was curious about her spiritual commitment. We had spoken about many different things, but not religion, so I decided to ask.

"Do you have a home church?"

"Not really. Since my father retired and left his church, I haven't attended any church on a regular basis."

"I think we should start visiting some churches to find a home church we can attend on a regular basis."

"That's fine."

Her response was less than enthusiastic. I felt she was taking a break, since she spent her early life in church three to four days a week, every week. I always considered myself a spiritual person, although I wasn't involved in a church on a consistent basis. At times, I felt guilty about it. Since I was going to be in town that upcoming weekend, I asked Marlene to find a church we could visit.

Over the following month we visited three different churches. We even attended the Love Center Church in Oakland and the service was amazing. Walter Hawkins was the pastor and the Hawkins family members were in the choir. It was like having church at a gospel concert.

I suggested, "We definitely have to find a church like this in L.A."

Marlene looked at me and just smiled in response. Finally we decided to join an L.A. church that had a balance of good music and strong messages. I knew that if my relationship with Marlene was going to flourish, we needed to establish a strong spiritual foundation. We had nailed the entertainment part of our relationship, but the Lord was imperative for balance, a healthy and ultimately successful relationship.

Time went by and Christmas had passed. J.R. spent his New Years Eve in L.A. He invited Marlene and me to join him and his friend at several parties. He leased a limousine so we didn't have to worry about finding each party or drinking. It was the best New Years Eve I've ever experienced. The Who's Who of the L.A. celebrity scene was in attendance, so Marlene was in her glory.

Marlene and I celebrated our one-year anniversary of officially dating, so I wanted to do something special on Valentine's Day. On one particular Sunday service, the Holy Spirit touched Marlene in a mighty way. She got very emotional and started crying. When the pastor had an alter call, she walked to the front to give a confession and receive prayer. This was an enormous surprise to me, because I'd never seen her cry like this. I didn't think to escort her because I was still dazed that she got up. A female parishioner grabbed her by the arm and walked her up. When the service was over I wanted her to know how I felt about what she'd done.

"I'm sorry for not walking you to the alter. That was a big deal."

"If you had, I wouldn't have noticed anyway. I was in another place."

"Wow, that was powerful. I didn't see it coming."

When I dropped her off at her home, she leaned over and kissed me. Her face lit up beautifully as she said, "Let's get baptized."

"Really?" I asked taken aback. "Is this something *you* want to do?"

"Yes."

"Alright. Let's discuss it next weekend in San Francisco."

That weekend, we decided to get baptized on Valentine's Day, which was three weeks later. I wanted to do something special on Valentines Day, but getting baptized didn't cross my mind. I was going to ask Marlene to marry me and give her an engagement ring after we got baptized. I decided to call my mother, then my dad to discuss my plan. My mother thought it would be a wonderful surprise.

My dad asked, "What took you so long? I thought you were going to blow it. Congratulations, Son. I'm sure she'll say yes."

"Thanks, Dad. I hope so."

The next two weeks were an adventure. I spent a lot of time searching for the right engagement ring. With the help of a friend back home, I decided on a one and a half carat 14k white gold ring. The price tag was twelve grand, so if she said no I would gladly take it back for a refund.

It was Valentine's Day and we were on our way to our baptism service. Marlene's mood was solemn but I didn't have a clue why.

"Are you alright?" I asked.

"I'm fine," was all she muttered.

The ceremony took about twenty minutes. Our pastor emerged us in the baptism pool, stating, "Being baptized is a sign that you have accepted Jesus as your Lord and Savior. This is accepting your new life seeking to be led by the Holy Spirit. By asking and accepting forgiveness, it will bring the death of your old way of life."

After the ceremony, we got dressed and were about the leave the church when Marlene asked the pastor, "Now that I'm a new person, are all my sins of the past forgiven?"

The pastor replied, "Yes, Marlene, you are born again."

The look on her face was like the weight of the world had just been lifted off of her shoulders.

As we walked to the car, I asked Marlene, "What are you feeling?"

She released a heavy sigh and replied, "Peace and joyfulness."

"I feel the same way. It's amazing." Once we were in the car I told her, "I put my wallet in the glove compartment, would you pass it to me?"

As she opened the glove box and saw the small box, her eyes widened.

"What is this?" she asked reaching for it.

"I don't know. Take a look and see."

She opened the box, looked at the ring and screamed, "James! Oh my God!"

"Will you marry me?"

"Yes–yes, of course!"

In the parking lot of the church, we embraced and she kissed me passionately. The rest of the Valentine's Day weekend was like a wonderful dream. She took me to my favorite Italian restaurant for a romantic dinner and surprised me with an 18-caret gold braided bracelet.

Both my family and Marlene's seemed to be happy about our engagement. However, Aunt Vera and staff members of the Ascending Media Group West who knew we were dating felt it was premature. There was one person who definitely wasn't pleased at all and that was Lawrence Allen, Marlene's ex-husband. My interaction with Lawrence was limited. I met him a couple of times when he dropped off the kids and he was polite. Marlene said when she told him about the engagement, he responded, "You can do better than him."

Marlene claimed, "Well, James says nice things about you being a good father and your extra help with the kids." I made every attempt to be respectful of their relationship but it was irrelevant because he didn't waste time becoming less cooperative inclusive of making late child support payments. He stopped being flexible in regards to his scheduled weekends to keep the children. I always felt he still had feelings for Marlene even though she'd been in relationships since their divorce. Until our engagement, she had never become serious with anyone. If it came down to excitement, exposure, and passion I'd win, but if it were a battle of financial resources, I would have lost by a TKO.

I was living a pretty charmed life. Other than the problem created by Nancy Arnett and her little crew, business was doing well and I was in a solid relationship. Nonetheless, over the next eighteen months, things changed in a major way. First there was Lawrence's attitude modification. He went from being occasionally late on his child support payments to a regular basis. I knew it wasn't that he didn't have it because his daughter never wanted for anything. Yet, it caused Marlene to adjust her monthly budget. Her travel to San Francisco was affected because he kept to the court ordered child custody schedule, so when an event was on a weekend that Marlene had the kids, he wouldn't switch like he had in the past. Marlene was a person who was used to having her way, so this new situation had an overtly negative affect on her positive attitude, which had been pretty good since our engagement and baptism.

The other issue was the slow progress that Ascending Media Group San Francisco satellite office was making. After a few months in operation, J.R. determined we needed to do something to jump-start the process of growing the business. The decision was made to have Jeffrey Silver, our L.A. general manager, to begin making bi-weekly visits and my role would be reduced. Normally, that would have been a blow to my ego, but I knew it was important for the office to begin contributing financially as it would enhance profitability for the West Coast operations. One of the reasons we hired a person with Jeff's experience was for situations like this. The challenge was that the media market in Los Angeles compared to San Francisco was like night and day. In addition, there were the constant harassing phone calls from the women identifying themselves as Sandra and Dorothy Morgan. J.R. informed me that there were two calls make to our home office in D.C., attacking my character and downgrading my job performance. The good thing was the company was extremely supportive. I had never experienced anything like that and if it continued, I knew I would have to do something about it.

It was June and things were slowly beginning to turn around in San Francisco. The only quality time I had with Marlene was in Los Angeles. We were still able to do some fun activities, however, she really missed her trips to San Francisco. Although, I told her earlier in the year that my children would be visiting in the summer, she'd forgotten. So when I mentioned to her that my kids were coming in two weeks, her reaction was disappointing.

"Sarah and Billy have a lot of activities during the summer. I won't have time to watch your kids while you're at work."

"I'm taking some vacation time while they're here, so I won't need you to babysit." I was disappointed and annoyed with her reaction and she knew it so she tried to make amends.

"James, you know I will be there if you need me."

"Okay. That's fine."

When someone is trying to show you who they are, pay attention for your own good.

Lauren and Daniel had a great time visiting. We went to Disneyland, Universal Studios, Griffith Park and Redondo Beach, among other family activities. Marlene and her kids joined us when we went to the beach. We had dinner at her home a couple of nights and I took all the kids to Fat Burgers for lunch one day. The two weeks flew by and although we had a great time, I was sad when I put them on the plane to return home. They seemed unhappy too. I got the feeling my daughter didn't like Marlene very much, but she never said anything or was disrespectful.

Later that evening, I called my ex-wife to make sure they arrived home safely.

"The flight arrived on time and they said the flight attendants were really nice. The kids had a great time in California. They liked your girlfriend's children."

"What about my girlfriend? What did they say about her?"

"They didn't mention her, so I'm not sure they liked her too much."

"Oh, okay. Have a good night and kiss the kids for me."

I was a bit curious why they didn't say anything, but I continued to move forward without questioning it further.

My father was my hero. He was a marine during World War II and was always there for my brother and me. My parents divorced when we were young, but he was always in our life. He delivered our child support to Mom every week and spent time with us. He was our Scoutmaster when we joined the Boy Scouts and my Little League coach as well. When I got divorced, I moved into an apartment in his two-story duplex house and lived there until I moved to California. He never remarried, however, it was my understanding from my brother that he was dating a younger woman. Dad was a real homebody, but this new relationship was making him more adventurous. The first example was his trip to visit my brother in St. Thomas, Virgin Islands. Raymond worked as a transportation consultant for the government. The second example was when Dad called to tell me he was coming to California to visit me. I thought it was unusual for him to take two trips in the same year, so he must have really liked the woman. In any event, it was a pleasant surprise and I was looking forward to seeing him.

When I told Marlene my dad was coming to visit, she seemed pleased. I told her he was scheduled to arrive the first weekend in December, which was a month away.

"He's welcome to stay at my house and use the guest room," she said. I was surprised with her response since she didn't make that offer when my kids came to visit. On occasion, when her children were with their dad, I would spend weekends at her house. I assumed that would be the case if my father was going to stay at Marlene's house. My dad had his own plans. He was bringing his girlfriend and staying in a hotel. Marlene was indifferent when I informed her.

I met Dad at LAX and I recognized his girlfriend, Ruby. I met her years ago. She used to babysit my brother and I when she was a teenager. She was about twenty years younger than Dad, but if he was happy, I was happy. The problem occurred when we arrived at the hotel room and they began unpacking. My father had two half-gallon bottles of Bacardi rum.

I pulled Dad aside and asked, "What's with the rum?"

"It's for Ruby."

"That's a lot of rum for one person."

"Yes, well I'll have a drink or two with her."

I was alarmed because my father contracted hepatitis as a young man working in a lumberyard. He was such a strong and healthy man that it took a year before he started showing symptoms. By the time he was diagnosed, he had suffered severe liver damage. His doctor told him if he wanted to live a fruitful life, he had to stop drinking. At the time, he wasn't a heavy drinker, so he had no difficulty following that edict. For the next twenty-five years, he didn't have a drink. Family and friends knew him as a teetotaler and never asked if he wanted a drink. So hearing he was having a drink or two with her was troubling.

"Dad, you've been so disciplined and healthy over the years. I just don't want you to hurt yourself."

"Son, I won't do anything I can't handle."

Dad and Marlene picked up where they left off from their introduction in D.C. She prepared a wonderful dinner and brunch on Saturday night and Sunday afternoon. On Monday, I took the day off to go sightseeing and dine out. I was sad to see them leave on Tuesday evening, but from all indications, Dad had a great time. I made two observations that worried me. I noticed that Ruby was a heavy drinker and Marlene was an excellent hostess when she wanted to be. Both were significant factors going forward over the next six months.

Marlene held an annual Christmas party at her home. It was an elaborate event with over fifty people in attendance. It was the first time I attended one of her parties. I volunteered to be the bartender. After the party, she told me she liked the way I interacted with her guests. Superbowl Sunday was another big date on Marlene's social calendar. Each year, she co-hosted a party at a couple's home that she'd known for years. I continued to learn that Marlene was a private person, but she did have friends who I would meet periodically. She didn't hang out with them often, but when she was around them, you would think they were her best friends. Slowly but surely, she began letting me into her world and it was interesting. The people I met seemed genuinely nice and liked Marlene. The next event was a barbeque for

Memorial Day in her backyard. The barbeque was intimate and more family oriented. Again, she seemed to love hosting and I saw her as a giving person who enjoyed being around her friends and family. I realized the events were structured, scheduled and nothing was impromptu. The key was that she let me see another side of her life. I determined since we were engaged for over a year, it was about time I was meeting people in her life. Maybe we could start talking about marriage, but life had it unexpected moments and sometimes the pain is unbearable.

I called Dad once or twice a month, but this particular call was the beginning of one of the most painful periods in my life. I called him around six in the evening. He answered, but his voice was muffled.

"Hi, Dad. Were you sleeping?" I asked.

"No, but I'm in bed. I just don't feel well," he mumbled.

My father never complained, so I asked, "Dad what's wrong? What's bothering you?"

"My legs are swollen and they hurt."

"How long have they been swollen?"

"I don't know. A couple of days maybe."

"That's not good, Dad. It sounds serious because your legs shouldn't be swollen. Call your doctor and see if she can see you tomorrow; you need to go to the ER."

His doctor treated him since he was diagnosed with hepatitis. They had a good relationship, so when he called the next morning, he was told to come right in. He was admitted to the hospital the same day. When my phone rang, it wasn't my dad. Instead, it was his doctor.

"James, your father is very ill and I suggest you come home so we can discuss his situation."

I can't explain the emotions that fled through me. That evening, I called J.R. to let him know I had to return home the next day because of a family emergency. I went straight to the hospital when I landed. Unexpectedly, they were discharging him that afternoon. I called his doctor and she asked me to come to her office before taking my father home. I had never seen my father so weak; he must have lost at least twenty-five pounds since last December. When we reached his doctor's office, Dad sat in the lobby. She told me he was suffering from liver failure because he was drinking heavily. His blood pressure was sixty over forty when she checked it. I was devastated and my dad was in no condition to go home and live alone. He was dying. When we pulled up to my father's house, I put him in bed and called his brother, Sonny. Uncle Sonny knew Dad was ill, but he was staying away from the family, so nobody knew just how sick. I explained that I was in town for a week and asked if Dad could stay with him and my aunt. He didn't hesitate. When we arrived at my aunt and uncle's house, they were shocked at Dad's condition. Uncle Sonny assured me they'd take care of him and let me know if things got worse after I returned to California.

I was depressed and exhausted. I called Marlene when I arrived at my apartment and she came over right away. I gave her an update on Dad's condition. As grief overwhelmed me, she wrapped her arms around me and held me tight. I had a lot of support from family members back home, the company, and Marlene, but none of it could prepare me for the call I received only one month later.

Uncle Sonny called and said, "You need to come home right away. We had to rush him to the hospital. He's in a coma."

"Uncle Sonny, I just spoke with him yesterday!" I exclaimed.

"Come on home, Jimmy."

I could hear it in his voice. I knew why I had to go.

It was eight when I made my reservations. I called Marlene to let her know I had to leave. I was astonished when she told me to make a reservation for her as well. She made arrangements with the couple that hosted the Super Bowl party to keep Billy and Sarah in case anything happened with Dad. I was truly touched that she was able to be with me at that incredibly painful time for my family and I. We took the red eye to D.C. and arrived at six the next morning. We headed directly to the hospital.

Dad was in a coma for five days. Family members, friends, and co-workers were in and out every day. Marlene was by my side for the entire ordeal. On Friday, a doctor informed us that they would like to perform a procedure on Dad, but they couldn't say if it would improve his condition. After discussing it with my grandmother, my dad's mother, we approved the procedure. The following day, Dad opened his eyes and began talking. Since he was in intensive care, we could only visit in ten-minute intervals. He wanted to know where he was and why we kept leaving so soon. Everyone was excited that he was communicating and continued to pray for a miracle. Marlene and I decided to leave the hospital for the first time, freshen up at Dad's house, and get a good night's sleep in a real bed. We were awakened at seven the next morning by the hospital. They called to inform me that my father had passed away earlier that morning and we should return to the hospital. We all knew that my father was terminally ill and it was a blessing that he woke up so we could tell him we loved him. I didn't have any words to describe my loss.

Dad came from a large family and was the eldest son so the impact of his death touched everyone. His neighbors, co-workers, and friends continually reached out asking what they could do for the family and how wonderful of a man Dad was. Everyone said he would truly be missed. I was in too much pain to deal with funeral arrangements or writing an obituary. Marlene was supportive and assisted with what needed to be done. She told us that her father was a pastor all of her life, so she'd been exposed to families going through difficult situations and tragedies. My emotions were all over the place. I felt guilty because if I had been living in D.C. still, Dad would not have begun drinking and getting involved with that woman. I was angry with my hero for letting himself get involved with such a person, especially after twenty-five years without a drink. But I was appreciative of everything he did for our family and that he wasn't suffering anymore. The funeral was scheduled for the next Thursday and all arrangements were completed, but Marlene did something that caused me to explode.

It was two days before the funeral services. My brother and I were running errands around the city handling Dad's personal business and closing loose ends. We returned home around four thirty and I asked my mother where Marlene went.

"One of your female cousins came by at one and said they'd be back shortly."

I glanced at the clock as it turned eight. It was hours later and I hadn't received a call from them. I was starting to get nervous. The cousin she left with was a little older than me, and was a distant cousin, so I didn't know her well. By eleven that evening I had no idea where they were. I was fuming. It was nearly midnight when Marlene finally walked through the door. She was unapologetic, indifferent, and reeking of alcohol.

"Marlene, where have you been? Why didn't you call?" She didn't answer. "I'm talking to you!" I shouted angrily.

"James, I'm a grown woman!" My family knew I was livid and my brother was standing nearby. I lunged towards Marlene, but Ray grabbed me and pulled me into my Dad's bedroom. Mom took Marlene into another bedroom. I had never been moved to such a state in my life and it was totally out of character for me. I have never struck a woman and I've been upset before, but not to that extent. After I calmed down, I tried to understand my outburst. Losing my father and the greed my family, including my mother, exhibited regarding my dad's possessions had a negative impact on me. Further, I was truly concerned about Marlene's safety in D.C. with a cousin I didn't really know. The most disturbing factor was Marlene's intemperate attitude when she finally got back. She knew the cause of my father's death. Her insensitive act of coming in the house, reeking of alcohol, displayed a new level of disrespect.

The next day was spent preparing for my father's wake. Dad's older sister scheduled a meeting with the pastor who would be delivering the eulogy so my brother and I spoke with him. Dad was a Christian, but he didn't have a church home. Reverend Miller was his sister's pastor and he wanted to speak with us to learn more about Dad. He said he'd heard wonderful things about our father and what we were telling him confirmed his findings. The one comment that touched the pastor was when I told him that I felt God awoke our father from the coma to say goodbye. He said based on God's love for his children and the life our dad led, my feelings were probably correct. The conversation with Pastor Miller was uplifting and comforting.

The wake and funeral services were remarkable. Mr. Thompson, the CEO and president of my company attended the wake and spent over an hour sitting and speaking with my eighty-two-year-old grandmother. It was a wonderful gesture and our family truly appreciated it. Dad worked for the D.C. Transit Authority as a bus driver and his co-workers arrived in a twenty-bus procession to the services. As well, he was one of the first minorities to integrate his Wesley Heights neighborhood in the early '60s. All of the neighbors who lived on his block arrived to the funeral in full force. It was amazing and indicated the love and respect my father generated. Pastor Miller delivered a powerful sermon and eulogy.

Although Marlene and I had little to no interaction since the Tuesday night confrontation, she was on perfect behavior during each service. She greeted family and friends with a smile and warm embrace. I thought, how could a person who acted so poorly the other night be charming, attractive, and sympathetic one day later. Marlene was definitely a complex person. On the way back to Dad's house, void of emotion, she informed me that she was returning to California on a red eye flight that evening and my cousin would be taking her to the airport. I replied coldly, "That's a good idea." I'm sure she needed to get back to her children, but I felt this would be the end of a doomed relationship. Oddly I didn't feel too badly about that possibility.

The Allure of a Predator

Chapter 5

Deceptive Intent

I was named executor to my father's will and I was responsible for settling his final affairs. It took me an additional ten days in D.C. to take an inventory of Dad's assets, get appraisals, pay final bills, and hire a property management company to handle his house. During that time, I didn't hear from Marlene and I had no interest in calling her. Each evening that I was away, I had time to think about our relationship. We had some great times together and I loved her children. Billy and I had developed a strong bond. I enjoyed talking sports with him and he consulted me on his training and interaction with his high school football coach. The coach was hard on him, but as I told Billy, he was developing him into an All-State player with the potential to receive scholarship offers from major colleges and universities. Marlene liked how I related to him, as Lawrence's main interest was Sarah, his daughter.

I went to California on a mission to turn around a failing business venture. With the help of outstanding new employees, that had been accomplished. I didn't have a social life and initially, I didn't have time for one. With my workload being greatly reduced, Marlene and her family filled a void in my life. I didn't have any friends or family in California and I found out early on that fraternizing with staff had negative consequences. Marlene came into my life at the right time and provided a wonderful diversion from my boring social existence in sunny California. We provided each other with the things we both needed in our lives. Marlene had the opportunity to experience fun activities involving concerts, plays, and interaction with media celebrities she didn't have when she was married to Lawrence. I was dating a beautiful woman who was a great mother, homemaker, party hostess, athlete and lover. However, with all this taken into consideration, Marlene had shown me, at times, a side of her that I wouldn't like to be around on a consistent basis. It was unsettling and alarming.

I was on my way to Dulles Airport for my flight back to California and I'd handled the major items regarding my father's affairs. What I took with me on that flight was insurmountable guilt regarding his death. He was only fifty-eight years old and if I were still living in D.C., I know I could have prevented that alcohol-fueled relationship that caused his early demise. Otherwise, my mind was on Marlene. I was convinced that it was over. Given that we didn't have any contact since she left, I assumed the feeling was mutual.

My first day at the office was comforting because everyone was supportive and congenial. I had been away for almost a month, but the general manager and business manager handled my workload. I didn't have to deal with missed assignments and a backlog of things I needed to do.

I returned from lunch and sat down at my desk when I received a phone call from the former love of my life, Marlene Hughes-Allen.

Her tone was angelic as she said, "Hello James, welcome home. I've missed you so much." I didn't know what to make of the sudden change in her personality. Before I could respond, she added, "I need to meet you this evening, so we can talk."

In my attempt to be hard, I replied, "What do we need to talk about? You said it all when you abruptly left after Dad's funeral."

"I know you're still upset with me, but if you give me a chance to explain my actions, I pray you'll understand and forgive me." Silence filtered through the phone for a moment before she interjected, "Can we meet at your apartment?"

"No."

"Why–"

"The Rose Garden at Exposition Park."

"I love that park, is six o'clock a good time for you?" she asked.

"That's fine." I said goodbye and quickly hung up.

I leaned back in my chair frustrated that I was willing to listen to whatever she had to say. The rest of my day was preoccupied with wondering what exaggerated story or lie she would conjure up. It had to be something worthwhile to change my mind about ending our engagement.

To my understanding, Exposition Park Rose Garden is the largest rose garden in the world. It displays beds of roses arranged in a grass-girded oval, around a beautiful central fountain. Located adjacent to the California Science Center in downtown L.A., it's used as a backdrop for several films and commercials. Marlene and I visited the park when my kids were in town. It's been called, "One of the city's best-kept secrets". Marlene was scheduled to meet me at one of the gazebos near the fountain. I couldn't have selected a more romantic place to end a relationship. What was I thinking?

Marlene arrived right on time, I liked that about her, and she looked great. She was wearing an Armani sleeveless linen flare-hem summer dress that accentuated her athletic arms and legs. I wanted to hug her, but I restrained myself and remained seated as she sat down next to me.

"I'm here to listen to what you have to say, but before you start, I have something to say to you. You really hurt me went you came in so late that night with such a callous attitude. I was going through the most difficult time in my life and your brashness was as if you couldn't care less or like you wanted me to get over it. Your actions were cold and heartless."

"Let me–"

"I'm not finished. Marlene, you were so supportive with coming to D.C. on the spur of the moment and staying with me at the hospital. You were great. But when Dad passed away, you changed. Initially, I attributed that to the grief we were all feeling. You were so close, then so distant, I was confused; but I couldn't stop to ask you what was going on."

"James, I love you and I want to start there. I was dealing with the death of your father, who I'd grown fond of. And when I called home everyday, I was getting troubling messages from Lawrence about abandoning my children. He hates to see me happy and he knows I'm very happy with you. Then adding insult to injury, he knows that Sarah likes you. I haven't been in a meaningful relationship since divorcing Lawrence and that was by design because he can cause trouble and aggravate me financially. I told you he's a control freak."

"Yes, you keep telling me that, but communication is critical to any relationship. All you had to do was talk to me. And that day you stayed out late, a phone call would have done wonders. I don't like surprises. If you tell me what you're dealing with, you would see how understanding I can be."

"I'm so sorry for my actions, especially when you were dealing with so much. I didn't want to bother you with my problems so I thought it was best to leave. Will you accept my apology? I promise I'll communicate better if you give me another chance. Will you?" I couldn't admit it to her, but she had me at, "I'm sorry."

"I love you too and I was thinking about how empty my life would be if you weren't in it. Let's sleep on it tonight and meet for lunch tomorrow. Okay?"

She nodded agreeably. We hugged and said good night. The Rose Garden was a perfect place to makeup. What was I thinking?

The following day began with a conference call. J.R., the corporate controller, Alex Gared, Jeff Silver, our general manager, and I had a lot to discuss. The agenda was the overall financial condition of the West Coast operations. Our company in Los Angeles was exceeding sales goals and the sales in San Francisco were improving, but to-date, the results were not meeting projected goals. J.R. wanted to know if our goals were too aggressive or if it was a personnel problem. Jeff explained that the sales personnel were fine and we needed to employ a little more patience because the Bay Area media market was more conservative. We agreed it would take another quarter to get a better assessment of the operation in San Francisco. The call took more time than I anticipated and my lunch with Marlene had to be pushed back. I called her and let her know we needed to meet at my apartment later that night.

The balance of my workday went smoothly. However, Jeff and I discussed the conference call. He felt corporate was being too aggressive in regards to a startup situation for San Francisco and they needed to back off their initial projections.

"Jeff, why didn't you say that on the call?"

"Corporate types don't want to hear excuses, we just have to make it happen."

Jeff's vast experience made him aware of corporate mentality. His instincts were absolutely correct, which was confirmed later that day, when J.R. called back to tell me the board of directors would not view a reduction of goals positively. I told him I understood.

On the drive home, I decided to stop and pickup Marlene's favorite Chinese food. She loved spicy stir-fried Kung Pao chicken. It had diced chicken, vegetables, peanuts, and hot chili peppers. It became one of my favorites as well. Marlene arrived at my apartment five minutes early and was pleasantly surprised when she spotted her favorite meal in the kitchen. She had a surprise for me in her hand.

"Is that your overnight bag?" She nodded with a sexy grin. "Aren't you being a little presumptuous?"

"Whatever you decide about our relationship is what it is. I decided I'd rather stay at a hotel or with you. Going home depressed isn't an option."

The previous evening, she gave me an uninterrupted opportunity to express my concerns. After hearing her explanation, I couldn't deny her a second chance.

"Marlene, if you forgive me for being insensitive to your needs, I will forgive you." The other major factor in forgiving her was because I loved her.

"You're forgiven," she said with a wide smile. "Now does that mean I can cancel my hotel reservations?"

We both laughed and I responded, "Of course. Let's eat."

Marlene and I spent the remainder of the evening talking about her kids, her sorry ex-husband and my conference call. She said Lawrence was really giving her a hard time regarding child support payments and she'd probably have to take him to court. That was something she had to do several times over the years. It was around ten when we decide to go to bed. She came out of the bathroom in a very sexy satin red baby doll jumpsuit. She looked hot and she knew it. Our sex life hadn't been active and she seemed interested in catching up for lost time.

As she slipped underneath the sheets she asked, "James are you familiar with Kama Sutra?"

"Well, I know its sexual positions developed in India, but to be honest, I'm not aware of all of them."

"I've been reading a book that explains the positions with pictures and I saw a couple that looked interesting." This woman was full of surprises.

"I've always been an excellent student, so I'm ready to learn."

It was a wild night and I went to Barnes and Noble the next day to buy the book.

We planned to meet on Sunday at church. When I was in town, we went to church on a consistent basis, as we enjoyed the message and music.

After service, Marlene suggested we go to her house so she could make brunch and talk about our plans for the future. Typically, we went to a local restaurant so that was breaking our normal routine, but I agreed.

"That sounds like a good idea. I've been thinking about our future as well. They say great minds think alike so brunch at your house works for me."

Marlene prepared bacon and spinach quiche the night before. We ate it with a fresh fruit salad, baguettes and mimosas. While we were eating, we discussed the church service and the powerful message from Matthew 7. The sermon dealt with judgment, grace, mercy and obedience. We both highlighted the text, "Ask, and it will be given to you; seek, and you will find; knock, and it will be opened to you" (Matthew 7:7). The sermon struck a nerve with Marlene and the conversation that followed brunch was straightforward and heartfelt.

She told me that she had lived a guarded adult life. She was a private person, which I knew, who only had a few close friends. She never let anyone get as close to her and her children as she had with me. Her love life had been limited after her divorce and she didn't want me to get the impression that she was a loose, wild woman, based upon our sexual interaction. She described herself to be a sensual person and claimed that I was the only person that made her feel comfortable enough to explore her sexuality. Her religious upbringing caused her to begin feeling guilty about that aspect of our relationship.

She said, "I realize we're engaged and I know you love me, but we haven't set a wedding date and fornication is a sin."

"Since we got baptized and engaged, my feelings are similar to yours. The fact that we've found a church and are attending services on a regular basis, makes your point quite persuasive."

"Fornication is a sin and the only remedy is to set a date and get married." She quickly replied, "James, I'm not trying to pressure you into marrying me, but if we are serious about our relationship and truly love each other, as we claim, it's the right thing to do in God's eyes."

"I agree. So when do you want to get married?"

Her beautiful eyes had a spark in them and her expression was breathtaking.

"October or November would be a good time. It's only five or six months away. But I think you should move in with my kids and I. Then, we can see how it'll be living together before we make it official."

I was overwhelmed; Marlene laid some heavy stuff on me and moving in with the family before we got married was quite unexpected. Based on how her ex-husband had been treating her lately, I couldn't see him acting any better with another man living in the same house as his daughter. It had become evident that Lawrence had little interest in his stepson. As Billy had gotten older, on weekends when Sarah was with her father, he stayed with his grandmother.

"Marlene, how do you think Lawrence will react when he finds out that I'm moving in?"

"I don't care about Lawrence's reaction. I'm taking him to court anyway. He's consistently late on his child support payments." She cut her eyes at me and said, "Lawrence doesn't want to mess with me. I know everything about his business deals and he won't want to get on my bad side. He knows it'll cause him major problems."

I didn't know what that meant and to be honest, I didn't want to know, but it sounded premeditated and threatening.

"When is a good time to move in?"

"In a couple of months."

"Alright then. I'll start making plans this week."

"That's great," she said.

The remainder of the conversation was spent talking about Marlene's background. During the conversation I asked about Billy's mother and the fact I had never met her.

"Billy graduated from middle school and celebrated a few birthdays, but his mother hasn't made any appearances. Las Vegas isn't that far away. How does Billy feel about that?"

I sensed Marlene wanted to be careful with her response, "Billy knows how his mother is. They speak and she sends him money on special occasions."

"Really?"

Marlene abruptly added, "I don't like talking about my sister. I think she's irresponsible and she should do better by her son."

It was obvious that was a sore point for Marlene, so I stopped asking questions about that mysterious sister. Marlene told me Lawrence would be bringing Sarah home soon and she needed to have a serious conversation with him. I took that as my queue to say good night and head home.

On my drive home I had a lot of emotions spinning in my head. Marlene was good at doing that to me. First, she told me no sex until we're married right after having a sexually explicit night. Would moving in early prove I'm serious? And would making love be okay? Or would she make me sleep in the guest room, especially when the kids were home? Obviously I had sex on my mind and her introduction of Kama Sutra to me wasn't helping. But, what lingered were serious concerns about her ex-husband and his reaction to a man moving into the house before we were legally married. I have to admit, when Marlene mentioned her knowledge of his business dealings, I found it disconcerting. Was he involved in something illegal? Was his business a cover for something else he was doing? Marlene shared so much information with me, but I still had many questions.

Marlene called me later that evening to tell me good night and to see how I felt about our conversation earlier. I told her I was excited about setting a wedding date and I would like to do it sooner than later. I mentioned jokingly, "Hey, can I redecorate the guest room since that's where I'll be sleeping before we get married?"

She laughed and said "James you're so silly. We know fornication is a sin, so we just have to ask God for forgiveness." She continued, "I had a serious conversation with my father about sin a month before we were baptized. He told me if I sincerely repented and asked God to forgive me for my sins, He would answer. That's why I felt at peace the morning of our baptism. Then when you surprised me with the engagement ring, I knew God was beginning to answer my prayers."

Faith and obedience is a serious matter, but I must admit I did like her response. God knew our hearts and we would be married in a few months.

"Alright. I'll give notice to my apartment management that I'll be moving."

"Great! And by the way, Lawrence gave me the money he owed me after we talked about some things. At this point, he knows where I'm coming from."

"Wow, that must have been some conversation."

"It was. Good night James, I love you," she said as she hung up.

I called my apartment management and gave them a sixty-day notice that I would be moving. Marlene and I discussed who should know about our plans. We agreed to tell our parents and her children. That meant we wouldn't be sharing the news with people at work.

Marlene told me she finally got an assignment as a private duty nurse. She would be caring for an elderly woman who lived in Brentwood, too. Her patient was an eighty-five-year-old woman with a poor prognosis. Her family was told she had a few months to live.

"Isn't it difficult caring for someone you know only has a short time to live?"

She replied nonchalantly, "It's a job. I just don't get attached."

I rationalized that it must be the best way to cope with her type of work. She told me a while ago that most of her clients would be families with an elderly or terminally ill loved one who wanted to spend their final days at home. It reminded me of Marlene's demeanor when my dad died.

Marlene's new position began at eight in the morning and ran until six that evening on the weekdays. This caused our time together to become even more limited. Weekends were the only quality time we had together and in most cases, they were spent with Sarah and Billy participating in their activities. Our weekends in San Francisco ended long ago. I guess this was preparing me for marriage and family life. It was obvious we both missed our trips to San Francisco because it was a fun part of our relationship.

My move to Marlene's home went smoothly. Since I lived in a furnished apartment, my clothes were the only major items to move. I had an extensive wardrobe and so did Marlene. She decided that my clothes would stay in the guest room and one of Billy's closets. I felt some of my things could be placed in the master bedroom closet; she had several outfits she rarely wore and some still had price tags hanging from them. Nonetheless, this was her house. I didn't make a big deal out of it. Once I moved in, she told me she had to notify Lawrence since he was the landlord. The only opposition he gave her was that he would stop paying the monthly mortgage since another man was living in the house. I wouldn't have felt comfortable living rent-free anyway. Marlene negotiated a rent of fifteen hundred a month, which was fine with me since my apartment was twenty-two hundred a month. The only problem I had with the arrangement was Lawrence wanted the payments in cash.

I told Marlene my feelings and she replied, "James, I'm happy his reaction wasn't hostile and paying him cash is a small price to pay in my opinion."

"Let's see how it goes."

Billy was the star running back on the football team. He was already attracting attention from major college programs and I was working with him on narrowing his options. On Friday nights, we attended his games, both home and away. Our healthy relationship continued to strengthen everyday. Sarah and I had a good relationship as well. However, we were more like friends and I don't think Marlene or her Dad appreciated how well we interacted. There was one evening that Marlene admonished Sarah for her overly friendly behavior around me. Marlene was a strict disciplinarian with her children and I felt Sarah was just looking at me as someone she could have fun with and make her laugh. I didn't understand it but I felt as though she didn't want me to have the same type of relationship with Sarah as I had with Billy. Regardless, I respected her decision.

The family was making the necessary adjustments for me to move into their space. I'm a neat person, which Marlene loved, and I wasn't demanding in terms of dinner, what to watch on television or with family activities. I didn't make waves and Marlene appreciated it. We decided to have a small wedding in November at a Lake Tahoe chapel. A month prior to the wedding, three incidents occurred that caused me concerns.

J.R. and the board decided San Francisco wasn't progressing at a pace to sustain itself. They were planning an end-of-year meeting to determine possible options and solutions. The next incident involved an unstamped envelope Marlene found in the mailbox. The handwritten note stated, "You think you have something special you don't there is no advantage to being connected with a person with such a negative reputation you can do better this man flerts with every skirt he sees and doesn't deserve anything nice in life!!!"

It was written in big print, flirt was spelled incorrectly and there was a lack of punctuation. You would have thought a third grader wrote the letter. Marlene and I concluded that it originated from the women I terminated. She didn't seem too troubled by the letter. I thought perhaps her ex-husband had something to do with it since our wedding day was quickly approaching. It had been several months since we'd heard from those women at the office. The last incident that happened was a call I received at the office from a local high-end women's boutique. The store manager called and told me that a woman just left the store requesting a line of credit using my name and Social Security number.

"My Social Security number? Who was the person?"

She replied, "Gloria Hughes."

"You mean Marlene Hughes, right?"

"No, Sir. She showed me her identification and it was Gloria."

I was extremely confused. "Marlene's youngest sister's name is Gloria, but how would *she* have my Social Security number?"

"I don't know, Sir."

"Well, what happened?"

"I told her I couldn't open an account for her without written authorization from Mr. Fairchild. Gloria–or the woman told me Mr. Fairchild was the manager at Ascending Media Group and it would be okay to open the account."

"Did you?"

"No, Sir. I told her she'd have to call Mr. Fairchild and as I was calling information to get the phone number, the woman walked out of the store."

I thanked the store manager for how she handled the situation and the warning. That was a strange call and I couldn't stop thinking about it. Why would Marlene's sister have my personal information and attempt to open an account in my name? If it were someone else, Marlene for example, why wouldn't she just ask me to open the account for her? I remember Marlene told me she didn't have established credit because her ex-husband had all of her credit cards in his name. Apparently, when they divorced, he cancelled all but one of her cards. I needed to speak with her, but if she were with her patient, I'd have to wait until later. I called home first to see if she was there, but there was no answer. I got home early to look at my personal files that were located at the bottom of the guest room closet. My tax returns were the only documents that had my Social Security number. It was a bit of a relief to see all of the records were in place. Yet, it didn't explain how or why someone would try to use my number. Marlene arrived home a little after six that evening.

After glancing at my expression she asked, "What's wrong James?"

"Nothing other than the fact that someone was trying to steal my identity by using my Social Security number. Oddly enough, the person used your little sister's name."

"Gloria?" she said with a look of bewilderment.

"Yes, Gloria!"

"Now that's impossible," she sighed. "She wouldn't do anything like that, you met her. Does she seem like a person who would do something like that to you?" she questioned throwing her hands in the air.

"Honestly Marlene, I don't know. My experience in California and dealing with people has been bizarre–"

"James, I know you've had a hard time with the women you fired. And then there's that–that letter you received last week. I admit I found it strange–"

"But who has access to my Social Security number?"

"You'd be surprised how easy it is to get Social Security numbers and other personal information. I learned that from Lawrence. That's why I'm so private about my business and personal life."

"Can you just call your sister to see if she had anything to do with this situation?"

"Sure. I'll call Gloria, but think about this," she said pointing at me. "That office of yours has all of your personal information readily available with your new address, Social Security number, and everything else about you," she stated snidely as she picked up her sweater and went upstairs.

I had to consider hiring a private investigator to get some answers and give me peace of mind.

Our wedding was now a week away and everyone was getting antsy. Marlene wasn't her warm and cuddly self and I was on edge as well. I was informed that when I returned from our brief honeymoon, I had to prepare for our corporate meeting regarding the San Francisco operation. We planned to fly to Lake Tahoe Saturday morning and get married the next day. We decided to only take Billy, Sarah, and Billy's girlfriend Alesea. Alesea was an excellent student and young lady who Billy was quite fond of. More importantly, Marlene liked her. Marlene coordinated the activities before and after the wedding ceremony. The kids would then fly back home Monday morning and we would return to Los Angeles the following Friday. Returning on Friday was fine with me because I'd have the weekend to get mentally ready for the corporate meetings.

Marlene was a wonderful event planner. I was looking forward to what she had planned for our special wedding weekend and honeymoon. We landed at the Reno-Tahoe International Airport and took a bus to the elegant Lake Tahoe Resort Hotel. It had first-class entertainment, restaurants and shopping. There was a recreation center for the kids, health spa and a casino that was open around the clock for adults. Marlene reserved two double room suites that had all the amenities you could ask for. Located in the beautiful Alpine snowcapped mountains, it couldn't have been a more picturesque setting for our wedding. After checking in, we took a tour of the facilities to take in the small intimate chapel she reserved. On Saturday morning, we took a scenic ride on a gondola that was seven thousand feet above sea level. Afterwards, Marlene took Sarah to the KidZone Museum and I took Billy and his girlfriend on a M.S. Dixie paddle wheeler cruise. After dinner, the kids spent time at the recreation center while Marlene accompanied me to the casino. I complemented her on scheduling some great events for the family and I couldn't wait for what she had in store for us once the children returned home. We slept in separate rooms during their stay so I was looking forward to having some fun.

After breakfast, we separated so we could get dressed and agreed to meet fifteen minutes before the ceremony and walk to the chapel together. When we came out of our room, our mouths dropped open. She was exquisite! Draped in a formfitting, champagne colored, laced mermaid v-neck wedding dress. She couldn't look any more beautiful. Sarah was beaming from ear-to-ear wearing an orange and satin ball gown. Alesea had her Sunday church dress on. Billy and I were sharply dressed in black Armani doubled breasted tuxedos. Billy was a handsome young man.

His hair was short with waves and his complexion was light brown. Being a football player, he had a muscular, athletic build.

Much to my chagrin, everything went downhill from there. We got to the chapel a few minutes early. Billy was my Best Man and Sarah was the Flower Girl. Before the reverend began the ceremony, he told us the service would be available on audio and videotape. However, halfway through the service, Marlene started to giggle. When Sarah and Billy caught sight of their mother, they began laughing too. Billy attempted to stop, but it made Sarah laugh more. It got so bad that Marlene could hardly get out "I do". I felt they made a mockery of a sacred ceremony. I was actually hurt and a bit embarrassed. After the service, the administrator was preparing the paperwork and asked, "Are you interested in purchasing an audio or video of your wedding service?"

"No, thank you," I answered abruptly.

Everyone knew I was upset. Marlene tried to explain that when she gets nervous, sometimes she giggles uncontrollably. I didn't feel like she was telling the truth; I thought she was trying to justify her behavior. We all went to our rooms where they changed into more casual clothes. Since the kids were leaving the next morning, Marlene took them downstairs to spend some time with them. Trying not to ruin the day, I joined them for dinner later that evening, but my mood wasn't cheerful.

After dinner, we returned to our rooms and Marlene got the kids ready for bed because they had an early flight the next morning. I took a hot shower and got ready for bed as well. This was our wedding night and I had mixed emotions about how the night would go. I was still annoyed with what transpired during the ceremony and I think Marlene was annoyed with my reaction. Since I moved in with the family, our sex life was limited and there were several reasons why. Marlene's conversation about fornication, the closeness of Sarah and Billy's bedrooms to the master bedroom, and our work schedule were just a few causes. I eagerly awaited the opportunity to rekindle the fire we had earlier in our relationship and I was certain Marlene wouldn't disappoint. When she entered our room she went straight to the bathroom with a small bag. Twenty minutes later, she emerged in a black, sheer and lace teddy. She said, "I'm not giggling now." Any thoughts I may have had about playing hard to get vanished as soon as Marlene jumped in bed and on top of me. She was in charge that night! All I can say is that Marlene was in another world and I was right there with her. We made up for lost time and the giggles. We fell asleep exhausted in each other's arms.

The next morning ascended too soon. We had an early start to get the kids ready. Marlene and I were looking forward to beginning the five-day honeymoon. Monday was a day of relaxation at the spa along with an incredible dinner and show at the casino. Tuesday started off well as we ordered breakfast in bed and my sexy wife offered "Coffee, tea or me?" I took her. That afternoon we visited Vikingsholm Castle; it was an interesting and historic place to explore. The scenic route leading to the castle was beautiful. The view of the crystal clear blue Emerald Bay paired with the snow-capped mountains was breathtaking. As the day was drawing to a close, we noticed the temperature dropping and the sky becoming overcast. Upon returning to our room and turning on the television, the weather forecast for late

Wednesday and the remainder of the week predicted eight inches or more of snow. It was early November in Lake Tahoe, so a forecast like that wasn't uncommon. Marlene and I visited Lake Tahoe the previous summer and I remembered the winding roads.

"I don't like driving on the mountainous snaky roads in good weather and this will make it even more treacherous."

"We're not driving now," she said sounding confused.

"I know, but if the snow is bad, we'll have trouble getting to the airport in Reno."

Marlene looked upset by my statement. "Are you thinking about going home early?"

"Well, yes. We can't take the risk of getting stranded and unable to return home on time. Besides, I have a lot of work to do this weekend to prepare for the corporate meetings next week."

Visibly upset, she snapped, "This is our honeymoon! These people know how to handle snow and I made plans for the rest of the week."

"I understand and appreciate everything you've done, but I don't want to take any chances getting stuck in Lake Tahoe," I explained, pleading with her.

She left the living room and stormed into the bedroom, slamming the door behind her. It was obvious she didn't want to leave, but my corporate meetings were too important. The company gives all newlyweds in upper management an all expense paid vacation to Hawaii as an employee benefit. J.R. considered that to be our real honeymoon. I didn't tell Marlene about those arrangements because I wanted to surprise her in the spring.

Marlene stayed in the bedroom for the rest of the evening and called room service for her dinner, which she ate in the other bedroom. I decided to have dinner in the hotel restaurant and spend some time in the Casino. While Marlene was pouting in her room, I made reservations for a flight leaving Tahoe on Wednesday. We slept in separate rooms that night. The next morning when I told her we were headed home on a noon flight, she began packing without uttering a word. I'd seen her upset, but I'd never seen Marlene in a state like that. She didn't speak to me on the one and a half hour limo ride to the airport or during the flight. When we got home, I carried two pieces of her luggage to our bedroom. As she began unpacking, she gently closed the door.

Later that evening I asked her, "Do we need to pick up Billy and Sarah from your mother's house?"

Finally speaking she replied, "The plan was for them to stay with my mother until Friday, so that's where they're going to be!"

"Okay. Well, do you want something to eat?" She didn't respond.

That night, I stayed in the guest room. I couldn't sleep because I was trying to determine what was going on with my wife. Intuitively, I felt there was more to it than me wanting to leave early to avoid a snowstorm. Perhaps Lawrence called her while we were away, giving her some trouble about Sarah, money or both. I decided that we should probably talk in the morning. When the sun came through the window the next morning I was in a more positive state of mind. When I entered the kitchen to grab a cup of coffee, my wife greeted me with a two-page, hand-written unedited letter. My mouth fell open as I read it.

My Husband,
Re: I Want an Annulment

I know this may (or may not) seem very selfish of me, but right now I really DO NOT give a damn about how you feel at this present point and time!! I'm sure this comes as no surprise about my take of your decision alone to bring our honeymoon to a damn screeching Holt!! I feel this is a pretty sorrowful start for our marriage to be made to feel second best to something that I know my intelligent husband is capable of making better if the case should arise of your choice of my wife or my job's happiness! But of course you chose the job! So go see if you can lay beside your job and get the warmth and satisfaction that I'm capable of doing for you! Let's see if your job can give you a nice "BJ" massage, touch, coffee, tea or me in the morning or anything that I, as a woman am capable, willing and able to do for you. Yeah a pay check is a good replacement but far from being warm and helping you feel tingly all over plus I've got a pay check too (package all rolled up in one!! Memories from your honeymoon is an event YOU can NEVER forget an lifetime event, but you my dear, you have made my moments something I WANT to FORGET!! Thanks for NOTHING!!

As I was reading this letter, I felt weak in my knees and had to sit down. This letter was reprehensible. I found it to be self-centered, self-indulgent and downright scary. Who was that person I just married? Should I call a lawyer or a psychiatrist? Oh my God, what am I going to do? Whatever it was, I needed to figure it out quickly.

Marlene left the house early that morning and I had no idea if or when she was coming back. I decided to call my mother. I knew Aunt Vera was at work, which was good because she would have advised me to call 911. As soon as I said, "Mom," my mother could hear it in my voice. She knew something was seriously wrong.

"What's wrong, Jimmy? Is everyone alright?" she asked sounding worried.

"No Mom, I'm not alright! It's been a disaster, beginning with the wedding ceremony right down to our return."

"What happened?" she asked sympathetically.

I leaned back on the sofa and recanted the chronological list of events that led to the madness. I told her about Marlene's embarrassing behavior during the wedding service and her extreme silent treatment after the impending snowstorm. But, the shocking letter this morning was more than I could handle.

My mother promptly replied, "God will not give you anything more than you can bear."

"I know, but this is crazy!"

"Jimmy, calm down and listen. Marlene had a special time planned for when the children left. People act differently when they're nervous. And laughing or giggling is sometimes a typical reaction. Marlene made sense when she said, "Those folks in Lake Tahoe deal with several feet of snow during the ski season, so a few inches of snow would not have prevented you guys from leaving on Friday. Son, I know you and you may have overreacted to the giggles and the snow. I'm not saying Marlene didn't overreact as well, but if you guys truly love each other, this too shall pass."

What a wonderful conversation. Just like my father, my mother was my hero too.

"I love you so much!"

"And I love you too, Jimmy."

I felt so much better when I hung up. I was prepared to have a heart-to-heart conversation with Marlene to see if she really wanted to annul our marriage.

I finally heard from Marlene early that afternoon when I answered the home phone.

"In a soft tone Marlene said, "Hello James, how are you?"

"How am I? I read your devastating letter this morning asking for an annulment, using crude language, which I've never heard you use before and you're asking 'How am I?' I'm very troubled and frankly, in shock!"

There was a pause before she spoke.

"I had breakfast with my best friends, you know, Larry and Rachel. Then I saw my parents after breakfast. We had a lengthy discussion about our weekend and honeymoon. I'm still here, but I wanted to call and let you know where I was. I'll see you this evening."

"You should know that your letter was disturbing in so many ways; I'm having a hard time processing it."

"I know and I'm–I'm sorry it hurt you. I was just venting my frustrations. My parents want you to come over to talk with them tomorrow."

"Your parents?"

"Yes, if you have time, and maybe they can shed some light on our family and me. I'll be home around six o'clock. I want to be there when Sarah and Billy get back from school so I can spend some time with them.

We can talk about my letter and bad behavior when I get home."

"Why don't you bring the kids home with you?"

"I think it's best if they stay with my mother until Friday."

We hung up the phone and left the rest of the conversation for later. Nearly a half hour later, I received a call from Aunt Vera. She told me she spoke with my mother earlier about my situation and wanted to lend her support. She didn't rub it in by saying "I told you so," but she did want to talk to me about how I planned to move forward. She mentioned the term, narcissism, and asked if I knew what it meant. I told her I didn't and she explained that a narcissistic personality is a disorder where the person believes they're superior to others and have little regard for other people's feelings. "James I'm not a doctor or know what's going on in your relationship with Marlene, but I think you should seek counseling if you plan to stay in your marriage."

I told Vera about my conversation with Marlene and that her parents wanted to talk with me. Then I told her I felt like I was married to the female version of Dr. Jekyll and Mr. Hyde. She could be so wonderful, but when Mrs. Hyde shows up, I'm caught off guard. The conversation ended with Vera telling me to be smart, seek counseling and don't try to resolve this situation by myself. It was almost time for Marlene to arrive home and I didn't have a clue where our conversation would lead; perhaps an annulment would be a blessing in disguise.

Marlene arrived with a big smile on her face and our favorite Chinese food for dinner. She placed the food in the kitchen and we sat in the dining room to talk. I let her do all of the talking.

"James, you have to understand that you're the best man I've ever met and everyone thinks you're good for me. Larry and Rachel told me they've never seen me so happy and my parents love your interaction with the children and me, especially Billy."

I listened as she went on and on explaining things some of which I didn't know. If I knew her better, I would have noticed that she did giggle or laugh when she's nervous. Then, she told me in Tahoe, she attempted to use her credit card when she took Sarah to the museum and it was declined. She found out that Lawrence had not paid the twelve hundred dollar bill. When she called, he told her to have her new husband pay the bill. That threw her off because she wanted to use the card to treat me while we were on our honeymoon. So when I decided to cut the vacation short, she projected the anger she had for her ex-husband on me. She felt we were both dictators who didn't care about her. I thought if she was going to project her negative feelings about Lawrence on me every time something didn't go her way, the marriage was in deep trouble.

She interrupted my thoughts, "James, what are you thinking?"

"You can't equate me with Lawrence. It just won't work because it'll be totally destructive to our relationship."

"I know. You want me to communicate my feelings and that letter was how I did it," she shrugged. "Obviously I need to learn to communicate without venting my anger."

Then I went somewhere she obviously didn't want to go. "Marlene, have you ever considered counseling for anger management?"

"No!" she snapped as if she was disgusted by the thought. My parents are all the counseling I need; that's why they want to talk to you. I'm sure you'll understand me better after that. Look, James," she said softly pouting, "I love you and want to be married to my soul mate." She abruptly changed the topic, "Now let's eat. The food is getting cold."

Relieved, I followed her into the kitchen. After dinner, we watched a couple of our favorite television shows and then got ready to kiss and make up. Our sex life was in full affect for the next three days while the kids were at their grandma's house.

I found the meeting with Marlene's parents to be enlightening and confusing at the same time. We had a nice lunch and the conversation was light, as we talked about our home church, current events and my children. After lunch, we went into the living room to begin our discussion about my marriage to Marlene and what she shared with them. Again, I let them do most of the talking. They cautiously explained that Marlene experienced a difficult childhood and was abused by her older siblings, which they believed was due to jealousy. Marlene was a beautiful child who attracted more attention than any of the other children. Since her older sisters and brother lost their dad, they had trouble adjusting to a new father and their younger sisters. Marlene became the focal point and outlet for their frustrations.

Mr. Hughes admitted, "I have to take major responsibility for the problems the children were having because I gave Marlene special attention to the detriment of their feelings. Marlene was a daddy's girl and I let everyone know it."

Mrs. Hughes added, "He has since apologized to the family and asked God for forgiveness."

"When I first met your family I felt everyone got along well and sensed they cared for each other."

"That's true," Mr. Hughes replied, "God answered my prayers."

My assessment at that point was Marlene's father spoiled her to a fault while her mother made little effort to provide more balance. Therefore, the older children took matters into their own hands and provided the balance in a negative way. Marlene was accustom to having her way and acted badly when that didn't happen.

Mrs. Hughes added, "Marlene married her first husband at a very young age and he continued treating her in a special way that was often hard to believe."

The examples her mother gave helped put things in perspective. A new luxury car every two years, world class vacations, a wardrobe that Hollywood actresses would envy and all the major credit cards. Her parents sought to keep her levelheaded and focused on God by telling her that all her blessings were from Him. During our talk I asked a few questions, but I had a clearer picture of Marlene and how her past caused her emotional problems. I was curious why they thought she divorced Lawrence. Oddly, they both felt she never truly loved him and grew tired of the material things he provided. Her mother maintained that he didn't give her space to develop, spiritually or emotionally. She said that's why Marlene loves me so much; she feels free to be who she is. If only they knew.

The one question that remained unanswered was when I asked about Billy's mother. Mrs. Hughes sat back on the couch and slowly began shaking her head.

Mr. Hughes jumped in and insisted, "That's a sore point with my wife and the entire family. Billy is growing up to be a fine young man. We've taken care of him since he was an infant. Lawrence and Marlene took good care of him when they got married but we've noticed the positive effect you're having on him. Marlene truly appreciates you and how you've filled the father figure void in his life. The children and Marlene truly love you and we feel God sent you.

Her family concluded, "James, Marlene is a good person who gets confused sometimes, but please know that she cares and needs you in her life."

Mr. Hughes ended the session with a prayer of encouragement.

"Dear Lord. Give James wisdom and perspective. Guide him according to your plans for his life and your commandments. Keep him mindful, Lord that your truth is and will forever be the ultimate truth. Amen."

I thanked them for their time and the prayer as I hugged both of them and said goodbye. On the drive home, I continued to contemplate the truth about Marlene's other side, Lawrence's finances and Billy's mysterious mother. Although they never addressed my direct question about her, I truly needed to know the truth.

Marlene greeted me at the door. She was excited to hear how the conversation with her parents went. I told her it went well and that I had a better understanding of her childhood and the challenges she faced. I told her about her father's powerful prayer at the end of our conversation. She said her father taught her how to pray and I must admit, Marlene did very well when I heard her pray at bible study. Marlene said she got a call from her client while I was away informing her that they had to take their mother to the hospital and the doctors felt she only had a few days to live.

"Are you going to see her?"

"No."

She didn't explain why and I didn't ask.

Since we were still on vacation, I decided to continue our honeymoon in L.A. We saw Kenny G at a local jazz club, spent a day in Palm Springs and had a great time at Venice Beach. However, what made Marlene's day was Friday night when I gave her fifteen hundred to pay off her credit card and buy something for herself with the remaining three hundred. I felt since I saved money leaving Lake Tahoe early, I could share my savings with her. Paying off her credit card had such a positive impact on her and I wondered if she had any other credit cards I could pay off. She screamed, hugged and kissed me for five minutes. Sarah and Billy were planning to come home Friday night, but after my gesture; she called her mother and asked if she could keep them one more night.

The kids arrived home Saturday morning and we did family oriented activities the rest of the weekend. On Sunday night, my mind shifted to the pending corporate meeting and how my role in San Francisco would be affected.

I received a warm welcome back to the office and was asked how the married life was. I said it was wonderful, not daring to mention or think about the nightmare in Lake Tahoe. I met with Jeff Silver to get an update on the big meeting scheduled for the following week. He informed me that J.R. had decided to have the meeting earlier and make it a weekend retreat out of the office. Jeff was to handle the implementation of a new sales strategy and I was in charge of developing the game plan going forward. J.R. didn't expect me to have the plan completed by the weekend, but he did want an outline on its components. In order to identify a course of action, I would start by reviewing the financial statements, develop different scenarios for fixed and variable expenses as well as complete a staff head count. Ascending Media Group was a small family-oriented company, so the possibility of downsizing staff would be an emotional exercise for all involved parties. We wanted to be a growing business entity, so coming up with a positive strategy would be mentally challenging.

That evening, I discussed my role in the weekend corporate meeting with Marlene and she was supportive.

"You'll do well. But the company is having a business meeting on a weekend and that's taking away from our family time."

"Marlene, this is an important meeting that will most likely determine the future of the West Coast operations."

Looking alarmed, she asked, "Will this affect you and your job?"

"It might."

She didn't say anything else. She walked into the kitchen to finish dinner.

The weekend meeting went surprisingly well. J.R. felt fine with our progress in L.A. and thought San Francisco had great potential. Jeff and I made our presentations and after a few revisions, we agreed to go forward with our initial plans. The major change affected me. Beginning in January, I would no longer make trips to San Francisco. My sole responsibility was to develop a proposal to be reviewed and implemented on or before June 30. I understood the need for me to stay in L.A. and work on the plan. Jeff and the sales manager would spend more time in San Francisco increasing sales and staff training. I wondered how Marlene would react to the news that my periodic visits to San Francisco were eliminated.

I knew the exciting part of my relationship with Marlene were our trips and activities in San Francisco. I provided a sense of excitement in her life in terms of entertainment. We attended high profile parties, events, and got back stage passes to concerts. Most of the activities were in L.A., however, the real pleasure was coming home after being away on business. Being home all of the time would surely be another adjustment for the family.

When I opened the garage door and stepped inside, I could tell the house was deserted. That weekend the kids were away, so I supposed Marlene didn't want to be home alone. I didn't see a note, so I had no idea where she was or what time to expect the kids back home. When I spoke with her on Saturday evening she said she enjoyed the day with her mother shopping and having lunch at one of their favorite restaurants. She mentioned that she would probably skip church services on Sunday and just spend time cleaning the house then relax until I got home. I guess her plans changed, so I unpacked my garment bag and watched television. Lawrence dropped Sarah off and then a half hour later, Billy's grandfather brought him home. No one had heard from Marlene or knew where she was. She arrived home around nine that night, looking distraught.

"Marlene, what's wrong? Where have you been?"

"I don't want to talk about it!" she replied.

I persisted, "Didn't we agree that we were going to communicate better?"

"Ok. Just let me calm down and get the kids ready for tomorrow. We'll talk later."

An hour later, Marlene joined me in the family room to explain what was going on. She was having dinner with a friend when two women approached her table and asked if she was Marlene Fairchild.

She responded, "Yes. And who are you?"

She told me they began to defame my character and the company in front of her friend, which was embarrassing. Her friend had to get the manager before the women left the restaurant. I asked her if she recognized the women, but she didn't. She speculated that they were probably friends of the women I fired.

"This is getting out of hand. I'll call our attorney first thing in the morning to determine how I should proceed." I hugged her and said, "I'm sorry you were humiliated like that." Then the thought crossed my mind, "Who was your friend?"

"He's an old friend; one of Lawrence's former clients."

I left it at that.

I called our corporate attorney on Monday morning. She told me there wasn't much they could do since my wife didn't provide any information on the women.

She said it was really a personal matter since no one worked for our company. I replied, "I do. This is harassment. I'm an employee and it's affecting me."

Noticing I was becoming upset, she said, "James, I know you've been through hell with these woman, maybe you should hire a private investigator to look into this incident. You should call J.R. Maybe the company will cover your expense."

After hanging up, I took a few moments to calm down. I decided not to get J.R. or the company involved with this matter. I would take the attorney's advice and look into hiring a private investigator. I told Marlene I was thinking about hiring someone to investigate the incident.

Her demeanor was completely altered from the night before.

She said, "James, I don't want you to spend any money on this and if they try to accost me again, I'll just clock them."

"Oh, now you're a tough guy," I replied with a laugh.

From the look on Marlene's face, I gathered she wasn't joking. After dinner, I told her about my schedule being changed and that I would be based in L.A. exclusively. She took the news better than I expected. She thought it would be good for Billy to have me home more. It was rather strange that she didn't mention it would good for us. She had news for me as well. She received a call informing her that her client passed away late Sunday night and her services were no longer needed.

"They thanked me for making their mother's final days as peaceful as possible and that they would be happy to provide me a letter of recommendation."

"What do you plan to do next?"

"I'm sorry the woman died, but now I have time to properly plan for my Christmas party in ten days."

"Wow, I can't believe Christmas is almost here already. The last few weeks have been a whirlwind."

"Yeah, who are you telling," she replied flatly.

December was always a slow period in the media business. I had the proposal to work on, but there was no sense of urgency since it wasn't due until the end of June. Marlene's annual Christmas party was a big deal for her and since we were married, it was a big deal to me. This year I would continue to be the bartender, but now, I had to supply the wine, liquor and beer for the event. Marlene only used brand name libations and I had no idea how much it would cost until the final bill was presented at the cash register. Pricey was an understatement. Since I was more involved with the party planning, I had a better idea of who was on the guest list. Many of the attendees were current and former clients of Lawrence's high-end auto shop. Many were former athletes she'd met when she was married and stayed in touch with after their divorce. I found out Marlene was with the former running back for the Raiders when she was harassed at the restaurant. She continued to amaze me with her event planning and how she played the perfect hostess. It was like an academy award-winning actress who turned on the charm once the lights went on and the party started. We had another outstanding party and the few close friends of Marlene congratulated me on our marriage. If anyone saw us together and observed the way we interacted, no one would ever think we had a problem in the world.

Christmas day was always a big celebration in my family and Marlene's family was the same. Giving thanks to God, opening gifts, and enjoying an abundance of delicious food. We had just finished breakfast when Billy went to the window to check on the weather and yelled, "Mom, you've got to see this!" We all jumped up and ran to the window not knowing what to expect. Everyone except Marlene seemed shocked when we looked out of the window to see a brand new SL Class Convertible Mercedes Benz. It was silver with a gigantic red bow on the top. We went outside to take a closer look; the car was gorgeous.

We looked inside to view the red leather interior and finally Marlene said, "Sarah, get the phone so I can call your father and tell him to come get his car!" As Sarah ran inside, Marlene explained that Lawrence called her a couple of days ago and told her he had a Christmas gift for Sarah, but she might have to take care of it until Sarah was a little older.

I said, "Oh, Lawrence has jokes." Sarah was seven years old. Marlene seemed annoyed, however, I think if she could have pulled it off, she would have kept the beautiful car. Later that day, Lawrence sent one of his employees to retrieve it. I wondered what else Lawrence had up his sleeve. He'd been in Marlene's life since she was eighteen years old and he knew all of the things that would provoke fury.

That year we were invited to a New Year's Eve party at the Beverly Hilton, the hotel that has hosted many Hollywood award shows and best known as the home of the annual Golden Globe Awards. It was a Black Tie Affair and Marlene looked stunning. She was wearing a Carolina Herrera sequined-sleeve silk gown, with a slinky train skirt. It was one of those dresses in her closet that still had the original tag. While she was putting on her makeup, I took a peek at the Bergdorf Goodman price tag, which reflected nearly nine thousand dollars. I couldn't possibly maintain the lifestyle Lawrence provided and as she was putting on the dress, I mentioned that fact to her.

She responded, "Lawrence was always trying to buy my affection, like the car on Christmas Day. Material things only go so far. You won my love by being real and loving to the kids and me. So many people in L.A. are living a lie and have plastic personalities."

Her response made me feel much better and she was absolutely right, money can't buy you happiness. The crowd was dazzling with beautiful and flawless people. I was sure some of the women were wearing gowns far more expensive than Marlene's, but she still attracted attention in such an impressive crowd. She was a hidden treasure who was just experiencing her coming out party. I was a fresh face in the L.A. area, but frankly, I didn't care because I had the most exquisite woman on my arm.

Since I'd been in California, I found some of the men to be disrespectful and rude. I attended several events with Marlene on my arm and noticed that some of them would look her up and down like she was a piece of meat. It didn't matter if I was standing right beside her. Marlene always claimed she didn't notice, but I felt she enjoyed all the attention she received. We had a wondrous time and I realized those events really turned Marlene on, so once we were home, our love making sessions were amazing.

The next major event coming up was her Super Bowl party, which she co-hosted with her friends. However, there were two incidences that occurred before the party, which raised major red flags once again. I decided to call the manager of the boutique to follow-up on the woman who attempted to use my name to get a line of credit. Marlene told me she'd spoken with her sister Gloria, who claimed it wasn't her at the store. The store manager remembered the incident and said she hadn't seen the woman since that day. I then asked her a question I hadn't thought of the first time we'd spoken.

"Do you remember what this woman looked like?" I was thinking maybe it was one of the women who were harassing me. My heart dropped when she began to give the description.

"I remember her well," she stated. "She was quite attractive, about 5'6" or 5'7" with light skin and long, dark brown hair."

None of the women I had in mind fit that description other than my wife, Marlene Fairchild. I was devastated once again. I was at a loss on how to handle the situation and concerned about how she would react if I confronted her. Nevertheless, I couldn't let it go. I needed to address it so I prayed for guidance first. I called her at home and told her we needed to talk. I suggested we meet for drinks after work. When she arrived at the restaurant, I began the conversation cautiously.

"How was your day?"

"You didn't ask me out for drinks to find out about my day. What's wrong?" she snapped coldly.

"I spoke with the manager of the boutique to discuss my identity theft situation last month. She gave me a description of the woman and they have a video of the incident."

Marlene's eyes widened and avoided mine before asking, "What was her description of the person?"

I replied, "She described you."

"That–that's impossible. There must be some mistake. I've been in that boutique before and she must have me confused with someone else. Look, I'll go to the shop tomorrow to get things straight and I want to see the video."

To get a reaction, I told her that the store had a videotape of the incident, but they didn't, so I quickly added, "Marlene, that's not necessary, if you say it wasn't you, I believe you."

"James, I know you've never seen a picture of Billy's mother, but people who have seen us together, think we're twins. Maybe she was in town and didn't let me know."

This woman was unbelievable; she's asking me to believe her phantom twin came to town trying to use my name to establish a line of credit. I sat there and took a sip of my drink pondering how she could blatantly lie. More importantly, I wanted to know why.

"That doesn't sound feasible."

The fact that Marlene would raise that excuse as a possibility was mind-blowing. After one drink, I suggested that we head home and continue the conversation there if she wasn't finished.

"I'm over it! I'm calling my mother to see if Billy's mother has been in town recently."

The ride home was uncomfortable because her story had begun to unravel. I had a lot of things on my plate with work and one of the things I didn't think I'd have issues with was my wife. I resigned to the fact that Marlene needed counseling and I had to find a way to get her to agree to going. I knew I had to be involved with the counseling as well, so my thought was to seek advice from our pastor and ask him to recommend a Christian marriage counselor for newlyweds transitioning into a new life together. That Sunday after church, I scheduled to meet with the pastor on Wednesday after bible study. I called Marlene on my way to meet the pastor and told her I would be an hour or so late for dinner. After Bible study and my discussion with the pastor, I was more than two hours late, but decided to go straight home without calling. What happened when I got home was the second incident that confirmed our marriage wouldn't survive more than a few more months if we didn't get some sort of intervention. As I entered the house, Marlene went into an unexpected tirade using every bit of profanity there was. In between the barrage of vulgarity, she claimed she was upset that I lied to her because I was over two hours late and I ruined dinner. She spewed out language I'd never heard her use. I couldn't believe how well she used the profanity; the words flowed off her tongue like they were habitual.

I finally said, "Stop! You're unbelievable and your language is appalling. I'm late because my meeting with the pastor lasted longer than I anticipated. I'm sorry. The meeting was about marriage counseling and he recommended a woman for us to see."

"I told you before, I get my counseling from my father! I don't need to meet with anyone else!"

"If you refuse to go to counseling with me, I'm not going to stay in this marriage any longer. You're making me crazy and I can't take it any more!"

After taking in my reaction and angry words, Marlene seemed to calm down. She turned to the stove and pointed towards the pots on top of it.

"I made your favorite Italian dinner. I–I just wanted you to enjoy it, but the noodles got too soggy and the veal is ruined."

"Thank you."

"You didn't call and you always call, so I didn't know what to think."

"If that's the reason you went off like you just did, a counselor other than your father is definitely needed."

"I'll pray on it and speak with my dad."

"That's fine but regardless, Marlene, you need to make your decision very soon. It's been a long day, I'm going to bed."

Marlene slept in the guest bedroom this time.

The next morning she joined me for breakfast and told me she prayed and decided to go to counseling with me without discussing the matter with her father. Then she added, "Sometimes I can be a real bitch."

"Please don't use that language or the words you used last night around me ever again."

Marlene sheepishly replied, "I'm sorry."

I always considered myself to be a critical thinker and problem solver in my professional life, so now it was time to use that skill set in my personal life. My challenge was saving my marriage by finding professionals who could help navigate us successfully through the process. Remembering what Aunt Vera told me about not trying to handle this situation alone, I knew I needed help. I was on a mission to identify and contact those people. The pastor gave me a head start when he referred me to Sylvia Gordon, a Christian counselor. I called Ms. Gordon and scheduled an appointment for the following week. Next I had to contact a private investigator. Our company retained a local attorney to assist us with legal matters on the West Coast. I called Howard Miles to see if he could help me find one. Howard recommended Earl Carmichael, a man he previously hired. Mr. Carmichael was a former detective with the Los Angeles Police Department and he was recommended without reservation. Initially I wanted to hire someone to investigate the women who were harassing me and confronted Marlene at the restaurant. At that point, I wanted to add another element, which was Marlene's mysterious missing sister. I contacted Mr. Carmichael and he was available to meet me the next day at my office.

Carmichael was a large man in his mid to late fifties. He looked more like a former football player than a former L.A. detective. The meeting lasted over an hour and it was detailed. Carmichael was direct and to the point. He wanted to know everything I knew about our former employees and Marlene's family. I told him the family was candid with me about Marlene's childhood. However, I still had questions, especially in regards to my wife's sister who left her child for the bright lights of Las Vegas. Carmichael never commented or reflected any emotions as he wrote the information in his notebook. I concluded the meeting by providing him with documents that detailed legal actions the former employees filed against the company and me. He said he would handle the case and gave me his hourly rate.

"Your fee looks fair."

"I'm just trying to help people. I'm not trying to get rich. I'll get back to you in two weeks, Mr. Fairchild."

That evening, I told Marlene I scheduled an appointment with the Christian counselor and hired a private investigator. I didn't tell her that he was investigating her sister in addition to the former terminated employees.

"I was impressed with both of the individuals and I feel they want to help."

Marlene's only response was dry and her expression displayed concern. "Are you hungry? Dinner's ready."

I expected more interest, but at this point, I was happy she agreed to counseling.

Our sex life was limited to once a week, however it was always great. Marlene was free and uninhabited in bed and she appeared to enjoy making love with me. Still, I remained concerned because our marriage couldn't survive if sex was the only thing holding it together and we both knew it. A day before the first session with the counselor, Marlene told me she was looking forward to meeting Ms. Gordon. She felt this would be a new beginning for us and naturally I was encouraged.

Sylvia Gordon was a middle-aged woman who was a certified Christian counselor for ten years. She said she had known our pastor for several years and she respected him greatly. Pastor Davis told her we had been members of his church for two years and newlyweds; he felt we were a fine couple. We thanked her for sharing Pastor Davis' kind words and we were looking forward to restoring the relationship. We began by giving some background on our relationship and the fact that we got engaged the same day Pastor Davis baptized us. She thought that was a wonderful way to begin a relationship. We shared some of the challenges we faced since we were together, but we didn't tell her about the ugly confrontations. She handed us a counseling survey that she wanted us to complete at home, then mail or fax it back to her before our next session. She explained, "The survey is designed to help me understand who you are and where you're at in the relationship." The document would give her our view on love and marriage and it would be held in strict confidence, which pleased Marlene. Ms. Gordon said her goal was to help us establish a solid foundation and she closed the session with a prayer.

"Dear Lord, thank you so much for bringing me together with this couple. We know that You have a plan and a purpose for their marriage and we invite You, Lord Jesus, to forgive them of past self-centeredness and come into their lives and marriage. Direct their steps from this point forward and give them grace to put You and each other first everyday. Make their relationship a blessing to others. But most of all, make it a blessing to You. And let us all say Amen." Our next appointment was scheduled for two weeks later.

Marlene was in good spirits on the drive home and wanted to treat me to lunch. She said, "James, I'm excited about this consulting you talked me into and I feel it'll make our marriage better. By the way, I have an interview with another potential client. Please pray for me because I want this assignment. Besides, I need the extra money."

"May I ask why?"

"Since our marriage, Lawrence is only paying child support for Sarah. He stopped giving me the extra money for Billy." Before I could ask, she explained, "He's not legally obligated to pay child support for Billy."

I decided not to continue that line of questioning and save it for another day.

We agreed to begin working on the counseling survey after church. At church, we told Pastor Davis that our first session with Ms. Gordon went well and we appreciated the kind words he shared with her about us. He said she was an excellent counselor and he was happy to hear we liked her.

The survey was a long, five-page document. It was comprehensive and based on what I knew about Marlene. After review, she wanted no part of it. She felt it was too intrusive and claimed she never had to answer questions like that in her life. She said Ms. Gordon was just probing and although she'd continue to go to the counseling sessions, she refused to complete the survey. I didn't know what to say. I didn't want to get into another argument, so I decided to call Ms. Gordon and tell her that Marlene was an extremely private person and she had a major issue with completing the survey.

"That happens more often than you'd think. If you're willing to return your survey, we can work around Marlene's missing survey and get some of her information during our sessions."

"I think that's a great idea. I'll get my completed document to you by the end of the week."

My workday was full with my normal workload and the increasing need for developing the proposal by the end of June. The first quarter advertising was typically slow, but even with Jeff Silver spending more time in San Francisco, the sales results were still pacing less than projections. My plan was to place consideration on downsizing or eliminating the San Francisco office. Jeff thought San Francisco sales would turn around in the second quarter. However, I had to consider and plan for the worst-case scenario. Layoffs create many problems, not only for the employees who are eliminated, but for those who remained too. If we decided to close the San Francisco operation, the revenue they produced would be replaced by increased sales in L.A. The increase in sales for the L.A. staff would appear insensitive and could be counterproductive. I prayed that Jeff was correct in regards to turning San Francisco around, which would be plan A or I'd need a strong plan B that would not have a negative affect on the West Coast productivity. J.R. required weekly reports on the progress of San Francisco sales. I had my hands full in my personal and professional life.

Marlene got her new assignment, but it seemed to be an unusual job for a licensed practical nurse. Her patient was a two-year-old toddler who had no physical ailments. I asked her if she would drop off some information I left at home by mistake and she brought the little boy to the office too. When I got home that evening, I asked her about her new patient.

"The boy looks healthy. What wrong with him?"

"Nothing."

I asked as gently as possible, "You're babysitting for his parents?"

She retorted, "I told you I needed the money!"

I quickly changed the subject. "Tomorrow, after work, I'm meeting with Mr. Carmichael. I don't know how long it may take, but I'll call you when I have a better idea of when I'll be home. Since our last flare up, I'd been conscience about letting Marlene know my schedule and giving her an idea of when I would arrive home. It didn't seem to matter because Marlene's demeanor varied from day to day. On some days, she was charming and playful, especially when we were around her kids and family. On the other hand, she could be impulsive or disconnected. I genuinely felt she was trying to be the person I fell in love with but circumstances had changed. I knew she was having difficulty adjusting to me being in L.A. full time too. She enjoyed our bi-weekly reunions and her periodic trips to San Francisco, but that changed when the company decided to have Jeff Silver do the traveling. I tried to schedule fun adult activities for us on Friday and Saturday nights but it wasn't the same as when we were dating. Lawrence's strain on her finances added more restrictions on her daily activities, which had a negative affect on her attitude. I tried to give her additional money, but because of my own financial obligations, I couldn't do it on a consistent basis. I was already giving her three thousand a month, which covered the rent and household expenses. In a candid conversation about her finances, she told me she took a twenty-five hundred hit when Lawrence stopped sending money for Billy. Before I moved in, she had an advantage because Lawrence paid the rent since he owned the house.

My meeting with Mr. Carmichael was interesting and I found he was good at what he did. After only two weeks on the case, he gathered some solid information in terms of the scope of the harassment. He found out about the calls to headquarters attacking my character. There had been four calls to the L.A. office by a woman identifying herself as either Sandra or Dorothy Morgan, three calls to my home and one call to a director of a student workshop at which I was a guest speaker. Additionally, he got a description of the two women who accosted Marlene. Sandra Morgan was in her late thirties, about 5'5" and thin, brown complexion, large ears, neatly dressed, and well spoken. Dorothy Morgan was between thirty-two and thirty-five years old, 5'5" to 5'6", light complexion, and slender. Then he told me that a woman in a red Mercedes Benz stopped at our house and asked Marlene's mother, who was just arriving, if I lived at the house.

After his lengthy report he paused so I could comment or ask questions and I had plenty.

"I had no idea they called my house and stopped my mother-in-law. The description of the two women who harassed my wife at the restaurant doesn't fit the description of the women I fired either."

"I know."

"How did you get this information?"

"I worked with the LAPD for more than thirty-five years and I have a lot of friends on the force who owe me favors. There are many ways to get information. We use phone records, neighbors, company personnel, restaurant staff, and the gentleman who was with Mrs. Fairchild at the restaurant. I spoke with your wife's mother about the women harassing you guys, but I'll use another source regarding the sister who is allegedly living in Las Vegas. Once I schedule a meeting with Mrs. Fairchild, I will be able to give you a final report by the end of the month."

"I'm impressed. Thank you. I look forward to finding out more."

"I'll give your wife a call tomorrow."

"Okay, but call her in the morning because she gets out early on Saturdays." I left Mr. Carmichael's office and called Marlene to tell her I was on my way home.

"How was your meeting?"

"Enlightening and I'll tell you about it when I get home."

When I arrived home, I took one look at Marlene and figured that we would be in for the evening. This was the weekend the kids were away. Generally, if we didn't have any major events to attend, we would grab a bite to eat and go to a movie on Friday night. Saturday night was our stay-at-home night. Since Marlene was wearing her silk and cashmere turtleneck and long leggings, I could tell she was in for the night. When I opened the door, a wonderful aroma that permeated the entire house was simply mouthwatering. Marlene cooked my favorite Italian dish, Veal Marsala, once again. It was prepared with Marsala wine sauce loaded with mushrooms and scallions. It was going to be a special night. While we were having dinner, she asked about my meeting. Not wanting to say anything that might spoil the mood, I only praised Mr. Carmichael on his thoroughness and the identification of the women who confronted her at the restaurant. I made it a point not to mention the calls to the house or his contact with her mother. She seemed satisfied with the limited information I shared; maybe she didn't want to ruin the mood either.

After dinner, she said she had a surprise for me. I followed her into the family room and she pulled a video out of her bag. It was a triple x-rated movie that she borrowed from her best friends, Larry and Rachel Hill. Marlene said Rachel was the person who introduced her to sex toys. I eagerly went upstairs to shower and put on something casual. The movie would be the prelude to our sensual night at home.

The next morning, Mr. Carmichael called at nine to speak with Marlene. They agreed to meet the following Wednesday evening at six. I arrived home just as Mr. Carmichael and Marlene were ending the meeting. He told me based upon the information Marlene provided; he would have the final report to me by close of business on Monday. I was pleasantly surprised with the speed in which he completed his investigation and I was looking forward to hearing the conclusion.

Mr. Carmichael met me at my attorney's office; I didn't want to meet at my office since this was a personal matter. The information he discovered was nothing less than mind-blowing. In summary, he could not find any evidence that Marlene had another sister living in Las Vegas or anywhere else for that matter. Billy was, in fact, Marlene's son who she gave birth to when she was sixteen years old. In an attempt to protect the family's image in the church community, her parent's sent her to an out-of-state institution that handled embarrassing teen pregnancies. If that wasn't enough, he discovered that Pastor Hughes was not Marlene's biological father. To avoid a scandal of epic proportion, Pastor Hughes married Marlene mother. They were already engaged at the time Marlene's mother told him she was three months pregnant. The problem was that she had an affair with a well-known community organizer who she had dated after the death of her first husband, Bernard "Red" Lee. Bernard was Marlene's real father. Mr. Carmichael told me she looked just like him, which explained why Marlene didn't look like any of her siblings. When Marlene was born, Pastor Hughes embraced her like she was his own and explained to those who questioned her appearance, that she looked just like his late mother and his younger sister who lived in North Carolina.

I couldn't possibly take anymore of his revelations when Mr. Carmichael told me he felt the women harassing me were most likely hired by Marlene's ex-husband and not the people I fired. However, he needed additional time in order to be sure of Lawrence's connection because he didn't have direct contact with the women. I told him that wouldn't be necessary. I thanked Mr. Carmichael for his outstanding work and paid him the remaining balance he was due. I called Marlene and told her J.R. called and told me he needed me in San Francisco first thing in the morning to handle an emergency.

I said, "I have a change of clothes at the office so I'm flying out tonight." I lied, but I needed time to digest all the extremely disturbing information that landed on me like an atomic bomb. "I'll call you from San Francisco to let you know how things are going and what time you can expect me home."

Marlene replied, "Okay. I love you and have a safe trip."

She definitely had issues, but based upon Carmichael's findings, she had good reason to have issues. Denying the birth of her own son, inventing a sister as a cover story, the lies about her birth father by her parents was almost too much to handle. I continued to contemplate every part of Marlene's past that he uncovered. She married a diabolical man fifteen years her senior who used money, an unimaginable lifestyle and influence to keep her trapped and under his financial control. As if that weren't enough, I came into her life and offered her something different. I was a good, honest man who cared about her kids and was someone she could have fun with. The work I had to do to find the truth was making me feel dishonest. Finally, I came to terms with the fact that I loved her very much and I felt sorry for her. The loathsome and odious lies she had to live with would damage anyone's mental stability. She needed help and my full support, so I pledged to be there for her.

Chapter 6

Will Counseling be Enough?

Our counseling sessions with Sylvia Gordon ended after six weeks. The second meeting wasn't as smooth as the first. The main reason was Marlene's reluctance to share information she felt to be private. Ms. Gordon received my completed survey prior to the visit, so we spent most of the time on my answers. Although Marlene didn't complete her survey, she did answer some basic questions that weren't too intrusive. Her spiritual history was an area she shared comfortably. Growing up as a preacher's kid provided Marlene with a great knowledge of bible verses. Her ability to pray in public was outstanding. What she didn't want to discuss was the background on her family, particularly rating her relationship with her siblings, her childhood and her parent's marriage. However, if she wanted healing from her dysfunctional past, she had to address her issues sooner or later. During our discussion, the matter of finances was confronted. When Ms. Gordon discovered that our finances were handled separately, she said that would lead to more challenges in our marriage.

Even couples who don't have monetary issues, marriage link's you financially. That requires thoughtful decision-making. If you don't talk about money or decide who pays the household expenses and manage the joint bank account, which we hadn't done yet, is a situation that will lead to a heated conversation about money in the future.

Based on my brief conversation with Marlene about her finances, I knew she was already having difficulty with her cash flow because of Lawrence's decrease in child support. Carmichael provided the reason why he wasn't obligated to pay child support for Billy. Lawrence never adopted Marlene's son because initially, he was introduced as her nephew. I decided after this session I would open a joint bank account with Marlene and start paying our rent to Lawrence with a check instead of cash. As well, I applied for a joint Gold MasterCard with a ten thousand dollar line of credit. I didn't tell Marlene about the credit card because I wanted it to be a surprise. The next two sessions dealt with conflict and anger management, which I was pleased to note that they were areas Marlene wanted to explore. Ms. Gordon gave us some points to help us stay calm when things became heated along with a list of techniques to use in tense situations.

Marlene enjoyed those sessions because they gave her tools to use when her temper was about to flare-up. The fifth meeting was a recap of the first five sessions and all of us agreed that there had been improvement. We opened a joint bank account and made our first rent payment to Lawrence by check; he wasn't pleased but he cashed it the same day. At the conclusion of the meeting the counselor asked Marlene to give the closing prayer. Ms. Gordon always closed each session with a prayer.

"Dear Lord, preserve us from all those traps and temptations that continually petition us to offend You. Allow the Holy Spirit to guide us in all the places where You shall lead us this day and always. Please keep our thoughts pure and on You. Help us to hear Your direction for our life in the quiet moments when we study Your word and let everything we say and do be pleasing in Your sight. In Jesus' name we pray, Amen."

As we headed towards the door I said, "I told you my wife could pray well."

Ms. Gordon replied, "She sure can. That's a blessing!"

It had been a few weeks since I applied for the credit card so I called to inquire about the status. After I explained the situation to customer service, she asked me to hold while she checked the records. She returned to tell me the card was mailed two weeks ago and I should have received it. She verified my address before I thanked her and hung up. That evening I asked Marlene if she'd seen a letter from a credit card company.

"I called them today and they said they mailed the card to our address two weeks ago."

She replied with a straight face, "No, James, I haven't seen any mail from a card company."

Marlene was unusually quiet all evening and went to bed early. When I went downstairs the next morning, she was already up, sitting in the dining room. "Good morning, James. We have to talk. Do you have time?"

I reach for one of the chairs and sat down as I responded, "Sure, what's up?"

"Well, I lied to you about the credit cards. We did receive it," she said dropping her head.

"Great. I wanted your card to be a surprise. Where's my card?"

"I thought they were my cards and I used them to pay off my outstanding balances on revolving department store accounts I had."

"What?" I was sick to my stomach and breaking out in a sweat but I could tell there was more.

"I took out a four thousand dollar cash advance to pay back a loan I got from Larry and Rachel."

In less than one month, she used the entire line of credit. No anger management technique could help me now.

I exploded. "How in the hell can you spend ten thousand in two weeks? Are you crazy?"

Marlene ran into the kitchen, grabbed a large beer mug and threw it at me, just missing my head. It was so thick it didn't break when it hit the floor.

I furiously declared, "I'm out of here!" and left slamming the door behind me.

Thank God the kids weren't home. I couldn't believe my wife. What could possibly make her think the credit cards were hers? She didn't have any established credit, thanks to Lawrence and at my expense, I learned why. She was totally irresponsible in regards to money.

I went directly to my bank to close the joint checking account that I just opened. I discovered that twenty-five hundred was used from my personal checking account that impacted the overdraft protection. I discovered later that Marlene used checks from one of my new boxes of checks. I didn't know what to do. I called Jeff, who was in L.A. that week, and told him I had a personal emergency and wouldn't be in the office. My next call was to Sylvia Gordon, the Christian counselor. I told her I had to see her right away and I would wait at her office until she was available.

She knew I was livid, but she didn't ask me any questions over the phone. "My one o'clock just cancelled so you can come then."

When I arrived at Ms. Gordon's office, she hadn't taken a lunch so she let me in ten minutes early. "What happened Mr. Fairchild?"

For the next fifteen minutes I told her everything about the credit card and bank account, Marlene's family background, her nonexistent sister, and everything in between. Without saying a word, the counselor burst into tears. With difficulty regaining her composure, she said we seemed like such a nice Christian couple, but she sensed hostility under the surface of Marlene's public persona, which she couldn't interpret.

"I prayed on it, but the Lord told me to let it go. I knew you guys weren't being completely honest with me. All I can say is that you need to work on your issues as well, particularly your spirituality. And based upon my observations of Marlene and what you shared with me about her background, your wife needs to see a professional, clinical psychologist. There's one more thing."

"Yes?"

"The sooner the better." Finally regaining her composure she added, "I will continue to pray for you and your wife and I'm sorry I couldn't help you. You need help that is way beyond my expertise." Ms. Gordon didn't have a closing prayer that day, but she ended the meeting with, "God bless you."

Once I jumped in my car to leave the counselor's office, I decided to drive to Las Vegas. It was a five-hour drive covering two hundred and sixty-five miles. That gave me time to clear my mind and figure out my next plan of action. I turned my cell phone off after speaking with Jeff that morning. I turned it back on later to see if I had any messages. I had five missed calls from Marlene and three voicemail messages. Two were from Marlene and one from Jeff; I returned Jeff's call.

"Marlene called the office three times looking for you and I told her you were at a meeting with a client. I didn't want to tell her you wouldn't be in today. James, she didn't sound good. Is everything alright?"

"No. We had a fight and I'm going to take a couple days off to figure things out. Jeff, please keep this between you and me. I'll see you on Thursday."

Again, my emotions were all over the place. I couldn't discern whether or not my feeling for Marlene was real love, companionship or just plain lust. I had no idea where her emotions for me fell, but I had to try to ascertain that as well. I thought back to the last time I spoke to Aunt Vera about Marlene and she mentioned the term narcissism. At the time, I simply looked up the definition in Webster's Dictionary. I needed to do more research on the characteristics of a narcissistic personality and prayed that Marlene didn't fit the profile. I was halfway to Vegas when I decided to call Marlene's parents because I wasn't in the right frame of mind to talk with my wife. Mr. Hughes answered the phone and when he heard my voice I could hear his heavy sigh of relief.

"Thank God! James we were so worried. Marlene called this afternoon to tell us you guys had a fight and she hadn't heard from you all day. Are you okay? Where are you?"

"Yes, I'm okay. I just had to get away and spend some time alone so I could sort things out. Please let Marlene know that I called and I'll speak with her in a few days."

Mr. Hughes said he understood and that he would keep Marlene and I in his prayers. I thanked him and said good night. I arrived in Las Vegas at midnight and checked into a small hotel on the strip. I was mentally and physically exhausted and needed a good night sleep. I wanted to have a clear mind before I began my quest to find answers to my fatal attraction to a woman who had the potential to do harm to both of us.

I didn't sleep well; I tossed and turned all night thinking about what I was going to do next. I was going to take some advice from the Christian counselor. I'll exercise regularly, which I'd already started, find a professional psychologist and develop my spirituality by getting into God's word. I got out of bed at five that morning. Hotels always have a Bible in the room, so I began the day with reading Psalm 23. I found a pamphlet with a prayer so I read that too.

"Dear Lord, I will focus on Your love, Your power, Your promises, and Your Son. When I am weak, I will turn to You for Strength; when I am worried, I will turn to You for comfort; when I am troubled, I will turn to You for patience and perspective. Help me guard my thoughts, Lord, so that I may honor You this day and forever. Amen."

I thought it was a powerful prayer and it was just what I needed. I thanked God for showing it to me. I found the hotel's exercise room and worked out for forty minutes. Before going back to my room, I stopped at the front desk to ask the clerk where I could find the nearest library and bookstore. The clerk had a funny look on his face. I imagined most people ask where the closest casino or strip clubs are located. He told me Barnes & Noble as well as the nearest library was about two miles away. He handed me a map with directions. I wanted to get as much information about a narcissist as I could find and purchase a study bible.

I spent the next four hours at the library doing my research. I found two books I wanted to purchase. They were *Narcissism: Denial of the True* and *Humanizing the Narcissistic Style*. Then I found a fantastic Bible that had four translations in one book. It was great for me because I had to have a dictionary nearby when I read the King James Version. It used language typical of the time and was translated in 1611 so the passages weren't always clear to me. I found the other translations were easier to understand, making my new bible study initiative more productive.

My time at the library provided some basic information that confirmed some of the behavioral traits Marlene exhibited. A person with a narcissistic personality disorder believes they are better than other people and have little regard for people's feelings. But this super-confident persona hides a person with fragile self-esteem that is vulnerable to any criticism. One article detailed it as a battle of the false self against the true self. The false self is intelligent, virtuous and basically perfect in every way, while the true self is imperfect, insecure and likely to be hiding highly unacceptable behaviors or personal information about themselves. Marlene would clearly be classified as a person leaning strongly towards the narcissistic personality disorder, although she doesn't completely fit. My number one priority was to get my wife help before it was too late. While at the bookstore, I found *100 Prayers of Encouragement* that had prayers similar to what I read that morning. That book would become a significant component to my spiritual development.

I didn't have my cell phone on all day and when I checked it for messages that evening, I had two of importance. The first from J.R. asking me to call him when I returned to the office and the other from Marlene saying she loved me and that Billy and Sarah were asking about me. The kids were used to me being home every evening and Billy, a senior in High School would talk with me most evenings about his ever increasing scholarship offers to play football in college. I didn't return Marlene's call because I was still on a mission to find answers to the many questions I still had. The big one would be why a good person like me would get stuck in a relationship like that instead of calling it quits and moving on with my life. I decided that my research for the following day would be on me. I slept better that night, partially because I was already exhausted from not sleeping the night before. My new morning routine included reading my new Bible and exercise. After breakfast, I headed to the library to begin researching material on men who stay in abusive marriages or relationships. There were a lot of articles and books on women in abusive relationships that explained why some women stay. I was surprised to see there were several articles on men as well. Men stay for many of the same reasons women stay. Finances and not wanting to support two households are just two reasons. Additionally, we stay because of our children and self-worth. However, some of the reasons that are more exclusive to men are shame, not wanting to admit being subjected to violence and denial. "It's not that bad, I can handle it," and "The sex is too good to give up." Others include, "I'm not ready for that much change in my life," and "Marriage shows more stability to my employer," are simply more excuses. I found out that fear of letting the public know, "I can't handle my wife," is a big factor. Calling 911 to say, "My wife just beat me up," isn't easy for a man to admit either. I determined that the male ego and pride were the main culprits in preventing men from saying enough is enough and finding help or just leaving. Many of those excuses applied to me. They were too problematic. I had to consider that it would end badly if I didn't seek professional help for not only me, but Marlene as well.

I checked out of the hotel that afternoon and headed back to L.A. I called Jeff to tell him I was taking an additional day off and would be in on Friday. Then I asked him about J.R.'s call. He said he didn't tell J.R. about my fight, but he told him I would be out a few days to take care of personal business. He said J.R. didn't seem pressed and was just checking in. I ended the call telling Jeff I'd call J.R. when I was back in town and reiterated that I'd see him Friday. I felt the time away did wonders for my disposition. I was emboldened to find professional help to save my marriage and get to the core issues that were affecting us. It was obvious Marlene's past, as well as mine, would have to come into play. My next call was to Marlene.

She answered midway through the second ring, "James, I miss you so much. I'm so sorry for putting you through all of this drama. I want you to know that I've worked on a budget that'll allow me to pay off the credit card debt in a year and I've spoken with my father. He promised to help me."

"We can talk about that but I believe the credit card situation is just the tip of the iceberg. We need to have a serious conversation about how we can make our marriage work and for that to happen, we need professional help."

"Okay, that's fine. When will you be home?"

"I'll be back tomorrow."

I was fatigued so I stayed at a motel overnight. She didn't ask me how far I was from L.A. either. I guess she assumed I was too far away since I had to stop to get some rest.

After a long pause on the phone, she finally said, "I'll have someone cover for me at work tomorrow so we can talk as soon as you get in."

"That's fine, have a good night." After that call, I felt there was hope. She didn't push back on seeking professional help and she seemed genuinely happy that I was coming home. I was definitely speaking to the woman I thought I married.

The kids left for school fifteen minutes before I walked through the door. Unexpectedly, Marlene ran over to me wrapping her arms around my waist before kissing me passionately. Given the difference in her demeanor from when I fled only three days prior, I didn't know how to react or if her mood would soon change.

"I prepared breakfast; we can eat while we talk. And after we talk, let's go to bed, I've missed you," she added flirtatiously.

As confused as I was, I wasn't going to argue with her. Over breakfast, I told her about my concerns with her dishonesty.

"I believe trust is the most important element in a relationship and if I can't believe what my wife is telling me, I don't see how this marriage can survive." She kept eating and I continued, "Some of the things you've told me about Billy's mother and that she was the one trying to use my credit to open an account just doesn't make sense to me. I think–"

She placed her fork on the side of her plate, looked directly at me and quickly interrupted, "It was me, James. I was too embarrassed to admit it at the time."

I thought we might be making a little progress, however, I didn't want to mention any of the information that the private investigator discovered. I was saving that for when we were under the care of a psychologist.

"Marlene, I think we need to find and schedule a meeting with a psychologist to help us with our issues."

Candidly she said, "You mean my issues. Right?"

"No, no there are always two sides to a story and I think counseling would be helpful for both of us."

I didn't want the other Marlene to appear, so I quickly told her that I loved her and I only wanted the best for our family. I think the word family disarmed her and reminded her of my positive relationship with her children.

She smiled and asked, "Do you have anyone in mind?"

"No, I thought we could work on that together."

She liked my response. She grabbed my hand and said, "Let's go upstairs."

"If you're ready, I'm ready."

It always amazed me that regardless of what we were going through, positive or negative, it never affected our lovemaking. Afterwards, I studied her face and couldn't help but realize that she was using sex to conceal something more sinister.

The kids were happy to see me back home and asked how my business trip was. I played along and said it was fine. Billy told me he received a letter from Oregon State inviting him to a recruitment trip, but he was still waiting on UCLA.

"Billy, that's exciting! Oregon State has an excellent program. You should consider making that trip. What did your coach say?" I asked.

"He said the same thing as you. They have a really good football program," he replied with a broad grin.

I enjoyed being involved in Billy's college recruitment process. I played baseball and basketball in high school and then baseball in college. However, I was never at his level. I was a walk-on in college and didn't receive a scholarship until I made the team. Billy was talented and he was being recruited by all of the major division colleges and universities. He was only interested in schools on the West Coast because he didn't want to be to far from his *mother* and sister.

I had to play catch up at work when I returned. I decided to call J.R. back when I got to work, since there was no urgency in his message. I met with Jeff briefly and he asked if everything was all right. I told him everything was fine but I had to clean up some loose ends that developed while I was away. Jeff was going to be out of town the following week so I needed to speak with him regarding his second quarter sales projections for San Francisco. I planned to work diligently on my corporate report and Jeff's projections were a major component of my recommendation. When I met with Jeff later in the day, he said he'd work on the numbers over the weekend and added, "I'll get my final projections to you by close-of-business on Monday, after I run them by the San Francisco sales staff." I told him that would be fine and to have a good weekend.

On Saturday morning, I continued my conversation with Marlene; I wanted to see if she would like to conduct our search for a psychologist together. She responded with a phrase she used often.

"You're the brains of this operation; I trust that you will find the right person. Can you tell me the difference between a regular psychologist and a clinical psychologist?"

"I really don't know. The marriage counselor mentioned that we should see a clinical psychologist. I'll find the answer to your question and have candidates to review next week."

"That's fine," she replied, sounding disinterested.

"While I was away, I decided to become more dedicated in reading the bible. I want us to attend the weekly bible study classes at our church."

"I don't know if that's possible James. Between my job and helping Sarah with her homework, I can't really commit to attending a weekly bible study. Besides, once we find the new counselor I don't know how much time or when that will take place."

"That's a good point. Let's take one step at a time and find the psychologist first."

I recalled Ms. Gordon saying that I needed to work on my spirituality. That afternoon, I went to the public library to find out about clinical psychology and how it could help our marriage. I learned that clinical psychologists are devoted to understanding mental health problems and developing effective treatment for mental, emotional, and behavioral disorders. Meanwhile, counseling focuses on managing several areas of ones life, such as interpersonal relationships. They concentrate on obstacles associated with physical, emotional, and mental disorders. It seemed as if clinical was a more advanced form of treatment.

After my research, I felt I was well equipped to ask intelligent questions to potential counselors and hopefully find someone who could help identify our problems. Although Ms. Gordon suggested that I retain a clinical psychologist, I decided to interview counseling psychologists. At the time, I didn't realize the depth of my wife's mental health problems because I wasn't ready to see and address them.

The kids were home that weekend. We decided to rent a family-oriented movie and order pizza. Marlene made strawberry shortcake for dessert. After Billy and Sarah went to bed, I had time to tell Marlene about the results of my research. I gave her the definitions she requested, however I deliberately omitted the fact that a clinical psychologist placed more emphasis on mental health issues especially since I asked her if she was crazy when I found out about the credit card debt. I wasn't going there again. Overall, we had a nice weekend with the kids. I relaxed Sunday evening and went to bed early because I wanted to be well rested for a busy week at the office.

Jeff handed me his sales projections early that afternoon, which allowed me to begin working on revenue, the most important aspect of my corporate report. The sales projections Jeff provided were not as aggressive as I thought. In fact, I felt they were realistic. The problem would be maintaining the current staff and spending levels, based upon the projections. My focus would have to be Plan B. We needed to keep the San Francisco office operating, but cut staff and other costs. Plan C would be closing that office, which would add pressure on the L.A. market to exceed their sale forecasts going forward and maintain that production on a consistent basis. Jeff agreed with me, we felt we had to avoid closing that office at all cost. Jeff was confident that his new sales numbers would be attainable even with a reduced sales staff. He felt the best account executives should have access to more accounts and because of their superior skill set, they could turn the accounts into ready, able, and willing buyers.

On my drive home, I received a call from Marlene to remind me that her annual Super Bowl party was that upcoming Sunday. It was always a great event and I was looking forward to it. Time seemed to soar. That would be my third super bowl party, meaning I'd been with Marlene for over three years. That evening, we discussed my day and the report I was working on. I told her how important it was and that I wanted to complete the report before the deadline at the end of June. I admitted that it would probably impact how much time I'd have to search for a new counselor.

"That's okay. We want to make sure we selected the right person."

I agreed.

My strategy to find a psychologist was to contact the California Psychological Association and obtain a list of psychologists in our area. I discovered that the hourly rate could range from four hundred to nine hundred dollars per session, which was a substantial difference from the one hundred and fifty we were paying the first counselor. Cost would be a major factor, so I was determined to get the most out of my money. Based on the nature of the conflicts I had with my wife, a psychologist who had extensive experience dealing with anger management issues would be a top priority. Cost would not eliminate the right person, but it was a major factor in our search. I often wondered if all of Marlene's anger stemmed from her childhood or if there was something else. Lawrence knew how to reach her hot button by withholding money and I was beginning to see she still had some control over him too. She used Sarah as her leverage and the fact that he would take her back without a second thought. She used her looks, charismatic charm and sensuality to manipulate anyone to get what she wanted and it worked, as I knew so well.

It was Super Bowl Sunday and Marlene was already at Larry and Rachel's house making final preparations. This year would be the first year Billy was invited. The menu included the traditional party favorites, buffalo wings, guacamole dip, pigs in blankets and they added white bean chili, buffalo chicken salad, melt-in-your-mouth barbecued ribs, grilled sausage with spicy sauce and German potato salad. For dessert they made sweet potato pie, brownies and Marlene's delicious German chocolate cake.

Billy took one look at the food and said, "I'm going to gain ten pounds."

I replied, "Don't hurt yourself. Spring practice is in two months."

We both laughed.

The game was a blowout, so everyone seemed to focus on the food and good conversation. This was the first time I was able to spend some time with Larry. He was a civil engineer and lived in L.A. for over twenty years. He met his wife in California when he moved from Dallas, Texas. He met Marlene and Lawrence at the auto repair shop and remained close friends with Marlene since their divorce. He told me Marlene was raving about some guy she met and they never saw her that excited about anyone other than her children. Then he said, "She really loves you. You're a good man for her."

As we were cleaning up and getting ready for our trip home, Larry called me aside and said, "Let's meet for lunch, I enjoy talking to you."

"That sounds good."

"I'll give you a call to set it up on Tuesday. I have something I want to share with you."

He had my curiosity. Since we were in separate cars, Billy and I headed home before Marlene.

On the drive home, I asked Billy, "Did you have a good time?"

"Are you kidding? I didn't know what I was missing. The food was outrageous."

"Yeah," I chuckled. "They sure know how to put on a great party."

Marlene arrived about thirty minutes after us and I could tell she was exhausted. She had worked on the party all weekend. "I'm going to take a bath and go to bed. Good night guys."

Billy and I told her she did a great job and we enjoyed everything, except the blowout game. She smiled and inaudibly climbed the stairs and disappeared.

I wasn't ready for bed so I turned on the television in the family room to watch Sports Center. Billy joined me as the sportscasters attempted to recap the lackluster game. As Billy was sitting there, I started wondering about his relationship with his aunt or mother. I didn't know how much he really knew, but I was sure he couldn't feel good about a birth mother who lived in Las Vegas. She never celebrated his birthdays or his middle school graduation or anything important in his life. The other major concern was his biological father. Who was he? He wasn't close to Lawrence and I enjoyed filling that void, but the entire situation had to be confusing to a teenager. I admit, Marlene had a loving relationship with Billy and I truly believed the feelings were mutual. I hoped I would be able to get some understanding once we began our counseling. However, I didn't see how the truth about Marlene's past could be revealed without causing a difficult situation for everyone involved.

Larry called me early Tuesday morning and we scheduled lunch for noon on Thursday. My workload was challenging, but I was interested in hearing what Larry wanted to share with me. We met at a restaurant near my office. Larry requested a table in the back where it wasn't crowded. He began by telling me that Rachel speaks with Marlene often and she knows more about her than anyone. She knows about the problems we've had and that Marlene feels awful about it. The next piece of information took me by surprise.

"You know, Marlene feels that you're kind of pushy at times, which reminds her of Lawrence. That's what causes her to explode."

"Larry, did she give Rachel examples of me being pushy?"

He picked up his drink and replied, "She feels you're forcing her into counseling and you should know that she's a private person. She feels you are *insensitive* to her needs."

"Wow! I thought we were in agreement on the counseling and Larry–it's for the both of us."

"I know. But Marlene is pretty insecure. I'm sure you already know that was caused by her childhood and her previous marriage."

"Do you know much about her family background?" I prodded.

"Only what she's told us. But you can tell there was some damage done. Rachel and I truly believe you guys make a great couple and Marlene has never been this happy. She loves your relationship with Billy. Man, she feels you're the father he's never had."

I thanked Larry for his information and kind words. On the way back to my office, I thought about how disturbing the conversation was, especially the part about me forcing her into counseling. I knew she wouldn't want to be subjected to difficult questions, but I knew if we didn't seek professional help, our marriage wouldn't make it. Once I sat at my desk, I pulled out my list of potential psychologists. I knew more than ever that I had to find a counselor as soon as possible and I *would* be pushy about that.

Two weeks later, something happened that hurt to my heart. I was at my office when I received a phone call from the head of security at Macy's department store.

The gentleman said, "Mr. Fairchild, there is a young man in our custody who is claiming you are his stepfather and you gave him authorization to use your

Macy's credit card. His name is William Allen. Do you know him?"

I hesitated for a moment and replied, "Yes. He's my son, Billy, and I did let him use my credit card."

Of course that wasn't true. Billy was a high school senior about to receive a football scholarship from a major university. He couldn't afford to have a negative report on his record.

"Well, Sir, I'm the director of security and Billy was with two of his friends and our security guard felt they were acting suspicious. But if you authorized your son to use your card, we'll let him go."

I was devastated, but I realized his actions mirrored his mothers. I called Marlene to tell her what happened. Marlene and I arrived home five minutes apart. I got there first and went upstairs to see if Billy was in his room. He greeted me with, "I'm sorry, Pop." That's what he called me when he didn't use my first name. "I don't know why I did that to you."

"I'm disappointed in you. You only had to ask if you needed something."

When I heard Marlene return home, we walked downstairs to meet her. She abruptly said, "We'll talk in the family room."

She went to Sarah's room to check on her and to see if she needed help with her homework. Marlene entered the family room with a look on her face that I'd seen before; it was her other self. She began a profanity-laced rant directed at Billy that revealed a deep-seated anger towards him. Her tirade lasted about three minutes and I was a bit shocked.

"How can your ass do this to a man who has been the only father you've ever known? You are an ungrateful bastard and I can't stand looking at you right now!"

I sat there stunned and in disbelief as Billy looked speechless. I'm sure it was the first time Marlene ever spoke to him in that manner. From my own observation, she rarely raised her voice towards her children, so this was extremely unsettling. What Billy did was definitely wrong, but to say Marlene's reaction was unwarranted would be an understatement. When she finished, she told Billy to apologize to me. He apologized to the both of us and went to his room. She was still visibly upset after Billy left the room. I didn't think it was the best time to discuss the entire episode.

Regaining her composure, she asked, "Are you hungry? Dinner will be ready in twenty minutes."

"Sure. Take your time," I replied. A half hour later, we were all sitting at the dining room table talking and eating, like her tirade earlier never happened. I felt like I was in *The Twilight Zone*. This incident confirmed that psychological counseling was needed and maybe for the entire family.

Later in the evening, I asked, "Do you think you may have been too harsh with Billy?"

"No. He needs to know that type of behavior is totally unacceptable, especially when it affects you."

"But he's such a great kid and to my knowledge, he's never done anything like this before."

"The key phase you used was 'to my knowledge'. I know my kids behave well, but that's because I demand that of them."

Marlene was a disciplinarian, but she did it lovingly. That type of rant was totally out of character when she dealt with Billy or Sarah. As we were getting ready for bed, she went into Billy's room to say good night and I heard them laughing so I guess all was well.

Billy was a wonderful young man. Besides being a world-class athlete, he was an excellent student. What really impressed me about him was his warm and giving personality. I remember before one of his big games, a physically challenged student in an area designated for handicap students called out to him. Billy stopped warming up, went to the student, gave him a hug and spent a few minutes talking to the kids in that section. Billy was one of most popular students at school, but his willingness to stop what he was doing and warmly greet a challenged student was admirable. It reflected his true character. That's why I was shocked and disappointed when I got the call from Macy's security. That was the last time Marlene had to reprimand him. Billy never disappointed me after that.

I narrowed my search to three psychologists I wanted to interview. Although Larry told me about Marlene's reluctance to counseling, that issue never came up when I spoke to her about the candidates. She reiterated that she would go along with whomever I chose and I just needed to let her know when the sessions would start so she could adjust her schedule. After the interviews were completed, I selected a local university professor who practiced his counseling out of his home office. Dr. Snyder was in his late thirties and had high credentials with outstanding references. He specialized in personal and interpersonal functioning that impacted emotional disorders. I felt I had found the right person for Marlene and I. I told Marlene that we would meet bi-weekly and the fee would be one thousand dollars per month.

She thought that charge was high and I informed her that the fee was about average based upon my research. The meetings would start in two weeks, every other Wednesday evening at seven, which eliminated my hope to attend bible study on a consistent basis. I could sense Marlene wasn't excited with the news, but once again, she offered no resistance.

For the subsequent two weeks, I wanted to focus on the corporate report. I didn't know where the counseling would lead us and I didn't want it to become a distraction and impair my ability to complete such a major project. The sales in San Francisco were trending down slightly and Jeff finally admitted they would miss their mid-year goal. That meant Plan B was now the best option to pursue. Closing the office was on the table too, however that would have a major impact on our West Coast operations and negatively affect our L.A. office's production. They would have to assume the responsibility of making up the revenue loss by closing the San Francisco office. That was a burden Jeff didn't want to place on the L.A. sales staff as well as himself or the sales manager. My presentation had to convince J.R. and the board that downsizing was the most viable option at this time and closing the office would be too severe. Jeff and Mark Sullivan, the sales manager, agreed with my strategy and would provide sales projections to support my assumptions. My goal was to have the report completed and presented by June 15, which would be fifteen days early.

My relationship with Marlene was going smoothly since her last blowup with Billy and their interaction was back to normal the next day. I had the feeling Marlene was trying hard to be on her best behavior because our counseling was around the corner. Dr.

Snyder informed me that the initial meetings would be joint sessions and when he had a feel for our personalities and relationship, he would begin to meet with us separately. The combined meeting would be for an hour and the individual sessions were a half hour, so the monthly fee would remain the same. When I interviewed the doctor, I shared the information about our first counselor. Without being too critical, he said she was correct to refer us to a licensed professional psychologist, however, she was obviously too attached by showing her emotions and crying in front of me. I didn't share the information I had about Marlene's background. If he was as good as his reputation purported, he would achieve a breakthrough with my wife and discover the facts himself.

On our way to see Dr. Snyder for the first time, Marlene seemed uncomfortable and tense. She finally admitted she didn't want to continue counseling because of the bad experience with the Christian counselor and she was only doing it for me. I insisted the counseling was for both of us and for our marriage.

"James, you know how private I am and it's going to be difficult for me to open up to a person I don't know or trust." She admitted the only people she really trusts are her parents, Larry, Rachel and me.

"My prayer is that Dr. Snyder will gain your trust and help you and me with whatever issues we have," I replied.

Dr. Snyder lived in a charming residential community in the Cheviot Hills on the West side of Los Angeles. His neighborhood and house were beautiful. After he greeted us at the door, he took us directly to his office located on the first level. It was clear that this association would be all business, no tour of his lovely home or social interaction at any level.

Dr. Snyder was no nonsense and he began the session by restating his credentials for Marlene since it was the first time they'd met. He explained how he worked and why he used his techniques. He asked us what we hoped to achieve from our therapy and based on our response he shared how he planned to help us achieve our goal. I got the feeling Marlene was impressed with his presentation. He was a genuine, honest person, which she seemed to like. The atmosphere in his office was warm and comfortable and he made us feel hopeful. He claimed that the key to a successful therapy would be our openness by sharing our feelings honestly. He answered all of our questions and advised us that he wanted to complete four joint sessions and then begin our individual therapy. Dr. Snyder ended the session stating, "Establishing a positive, safe and understanding relationship with you must be accomplished for our work together to be fruitful." Marlene and I agreed.

Marlene had a completely different attitude, as she expressed positive feelings about the doctor. She said, "He made me feel secure and safe, so if I decide to share personal information about my background, it'll remain confidential."

What I found interesting was that she didn't convince me that she would be truthful when she said, *if* she decides to share. "The doctor needs us to be open and honest if this is going to work, Marlene."

"I understand that, but it's going to take time," she said, sounding frustrated.

Our next appointment was scheduled two weeks later. He gave us an assignment, which was to prepare a written outline of our goals for both, our joint and individual therapy sessions. He indicated that our goals would be reviewed during our next meeting. I felt good about Marlene's reaction and her willingness to consider talking about her past. It was a major accomplishment; it would definitely begin the healing process for Marlene and our marriage.

My outline included my failed first marriage, my relationship with my mother and although my marriage would be considered abusive at times, why I stayed. Perhaps it was because I didn't want another failed marriage, fear of loneliness or that the sex was great. At this point, my opinion didn't matter; I needed a professional assessment. The joint meetings went okay. Marlene was still being elusive about her family background. She discussed the hard times she endured in her youth and her emotionally abusive first marriage. She didn't mention her missing sister and her relationship with Billy. I confirmed that she was a great mother raising two wonderful children. In the joint meetings, I didn't dare bring up her profanity-laced outbursts towards Billy and me. I decided to be more open when the individual sessions began. I discussed being too immature in my first marriage and feeling that my mother was abusive to my late father when they were married. I recalled the big fights they had when my brother and I were kids. I told him that I always felt the fights were my mother's fault. Dr. Snyder took it all in without being judgmental or placing blame. He was always respectful and professional. I got the feeling that we, including our therapist, were ready to begin the individual therapy. I was ready to have more freedom to discuss issues that were too sensitive to talk about in a group setting.

At this point in our counseling, Marlene felt that Dr. Snyder was about to start bringing up topics that would challenge and even upset her. However, because he established an empathetic relationship with us, she was ready to address her issues. Time would tell if she was willing to be honest.

It was the first week in June and I projected it would be a hectic month. My corporate report was basically finished and I was scheduled to fly to D.C. with Jeff to make our formal presentation the third week of June. Billy had his final recruitment meeting with USC that month and afterwards, he'd make his decision between Oregon State, USC and his favorite, UCLA, who finally sent him a scholarship offer letter in late April. I enjoyed going through the entire recruitment process with Billy. Each school did their best to lure him to their university.

Due to my hectic schedule, I was only able to attend one individual session with Dr. Snyder. However, Marlene had the equivalent of three individual sessions. She used the full hour when I was away and her normal half hour when I returned. The doctor advised us before we started meeting individually that we needed to sign an agreement stating he could share information between us if it was pertinent to our relationship. He added a disclaimer that if there was something we didn't want shared we had to advise him in advance. Marlene signed the document and seemed satisfied with the disclaimer. Now she could talk about things in her past in strict confidence, without being afraid that I would find out. She didn't know that I was already aware of those things she preferred to keep from me. If she shared the truth with Dr. Snyder, it would be a great first step in resolving many of her issues. I remained hopeful.

The meeting at headquarters was scheduled early the second week of that month in the conference room. Mr. Thompson, the president, chairman of the board, J.R., our corporate general manager and the controller attended. J.R. presented the agenda and introduced Jeff Silver. The group was meeting him in person for the first time. J.R. knew what our proposal would be, but he didn't have a feel for how the group would receive our recommendation to downsize the San Francisco operation. Jeff went first with his analysis of sales and why we were missing our projections. He didn't make any excuses. He stated that San Francisco was more complicated than he anticipated. His bottom line was that by keeping only the best and brightest sales executives, we would improve their production and efficiency. My presentation involved cutting administrative cost and moving to a smaller venue once our lease expired. I distributed copies of the pro-forma financial statements I prepared which indicated by downsizing, effective immediately, we would increase our operating profit margin by fifteen percent. The group asked some tough questions which we answered adequately and although they agreed to accept our proposal, it wasn't with much enthusiasm. After the meeting, J.R. shared with us that a couple of people in the meeting were in support of closing the San Francisco office completely. J.R. didn't give us any names, but if I were a betting man, I would select the board chairman and the general manager as the naysayers. The next morning, Jeff and I headed back to L.A. relieved that the presentation was over and accepted. I wasn't greeted as a returning hero after that visit. On the first of July, Jeff and I flew to San Francisco to implement the changes and terminate half of the staff; which was always difficult regardless of the circumstances.

After things settled with work, I was back on my bi-weekly scheduled meetings with Dr. Snyder. I would meet the first half hour and Marlene would go last. I figured she felt by meeting last she would be able to find out what I said about her in the first session. I was comfortable with those arrangements and the doctor was strict about not sharing anything we didn't want disclosed. I was midway through my fourth session with the doctor when he mentioned narcissism.

He asked, "Mr. Fairchild, do you know the meaning?"

"Yes. A while back my aunt told me to do some research on that subject. She felt Marlene might be suffering from that disorder."

"Is your aunt a psychologist?" he replied.

"No, but she's been suspicious of Marlene since the day she met her. Doctor, I did do some research on narcissism and I have a basic idea of what it is, but the information was way over my head and I decided we need professional help. As I told you, that was our first counselor's advice."

"Marlene is exhibiting some aspects of a narcissistic personality disorder, but it's not severe at this point. However, it's something we have to work on."

"Did Marlene agree to share that information with me?"

He nodded and claimed, "She agreed that she displays some of the characteristics and she wanted you to know that it was something she wanted to correct."

As we were finishing my time, he said he wanted to spend our next couple of meetings addressing my issues, he felt he had identified.

I said with a smile, "Doc, I thought I was perfect!"

He returned a kind smile and replied, "That's one of your issues."

On our ride home, I asked Marlene about her sister who lived in Las Vegas. "Billy graduated from high school in May, he accepted a football scholarship to Oregon State and we haven't heard a word from his absentee mother. I think that's very strange."

Marlene snapped back, "What do you mean strange? You don't know what you're talking about! She spoke with Billy and sent him money for graduation and she plans to meet with us during Christmas."

"Really?" I said as I turned the corner. "I guess I'll meet her then."

"I guess you will."

This was a major problem for me. Marlene was still perpetuating the lie about a sister who didn't exist. I decided that I had to bring that issue to Dr. Snyder's attention. I must admit that since we began therapy, Marlene's disposition had improved greatly and I was feeling much better about the future of our marriage. I knew my question about her sister disturbed her, but once I changed the subject, her mood lightened and she was that charming person I loved by the time we got home.

I was looking forward to my next therapy session. The doctor was going to tell me about my issues and I was going to tell him about Marlene's imaginary sister. I even called him in advance to ask him if we could extend my meeting to an hour and I would pay for the additional time. Marlene wanted to leave her session at a half hour. We arrived early as usual. I'm anal about being punctual and suspected that was probably one of my issues we were going to discuss. To my surprise, therapy began ten minutes early. His diagnosis disturbed me. I guess you never know who you are until you see a therapist. He said I had symptoms of an anxiety disorder and was suffering from depression. I thought if I was depressed, his diagnosis wasn't helping.

My expression caused the doctor to quickly add, "Like your wife, it's not severe and it is fixable. Mr. Fairchild, based on what you told me about your family history, pressure of your job, the women you had to terminate, harassment and being married to a narcissist, I am optimistic about making effective changes because you realized you needed help."

He gave me some symptoms to see if any applied to me and there were. But there were several other symptoms that didn't apply to me. Dr. Snyder assured me that once the issues are identified, they can be addressed and eliminated. He added that my new exercise routine was important, but maintaining my intimate and sexual relationship with my wife was even more vital. He said there seemed to be a strong bond in that aspect of our marriage. He ended with a new assignment. He wanted me to start writing down my dreams each morning and begin bringing my notes to each session so he could analyze my dreams.

"I don't always remember my dreams."

"Do your best."

I didn't get a chance to mention Marlene's mysterious sister, but after hearing about my issues, that wasn't as important. The sister was a way for

Marlene and her family to cover up a teen pregnancy and a child being born out of wedlock. They were issues that Marlene would have to deal with eventually.

As Marlene and I crossed paths on her way into his office, she said, "James was the session *that* rough? You look extremely sad."

"Yeah, I guess I'm a little depressed."

While Marlene was in with Dr. Snyder, I began reading from *100 Prayers of Encouragement*, which I always read while waiting for Marlene. I found a Stanley Jones quote that read, "God guides through the counsel of good people." Dr. Snyder was good people and with God's help, we were going to be all right.

Between our jobs, Billy's recruiting trips, counseling and church, Marlene and I had very little time for one on one fun. I could tell she was getting antsy, so I had a feeling the situation was about to change and I was right. Although I didn't know any of her true friends other than Larry and Rachel, Marlene made it a point to know all of my contacts and how to reach them. That list included family members, business associates, friends back east, and my ex-wife. It didn't bother me at the time because I had nothing to hide and it helped her arrange a special birthday weekend she had planned for me.

It was September and Billy was starting his freshman year in college. The reason he finally decided to select Oregon State University was because of their promise to give him an opportunity to be their starting running back as a freshman. My birthday weekend was Lawrence's time to have Sarah, so Marlene planned a trip to San Francisco. She contacted my former receptionist, who worked for a major concert promoter and secured tickets to the Luther Vandross, Anita Baker and En Vogue concert at the Oakland Coliseum. The concert was on Friday night so we took the day off from work and arrived in San Francisco on Friday afternoon. She said she had a special gift for me. When it was time to get dressed for the concert, she gave me the birthday present. It was a beautifully wrapped, large suit box. When I opened it, my mouth dropped open. It was a Versace black buffed leather knit-trim bomber jacket with matching leather pants. I was blown away and when Marlene saw it on me, she was too. I must say that night at the concert I was attracting as much attention as my wife and she loved it. She looked like she was proud to be with me and the concert was wonderful.

Saturday was my actual birthday and Marlene outdid herself. We had lunch at my favorite Italian restaurant in Sausalito. Afterwards, we hopped into a cab and headed back to the city.

"Marlene where are we going?"

"Be patient, it's another birthday surprise," she advised in a seductive tone.

We arrived at the address she gave the driver. It was a place I had never heard of; Mitchell Brothers O'Farrell Theater.

"Oh, we're going to a play?"

"Sort of," she replied with a smile. I was entering probably the most famous strip joint in San Francisco. It was known for employing hot and aggressive women and the lap dances were only the warm up. It was divided into three areas. A movie theater which played adult films, a room that provided professional lap dances and another area called The Voting Booths that had curtains to provide private alone time with your favorite dancer. Marlene seemed more excited than me as we experienced each section with an attractive young performer who we selected as our escort. It was obvious that there was a mutual attraction so she made sure Marlene participated or allowed all activities. After spending over three hours in that place, we could not wait to get back to the privacy of our hotel room to continue where we left off at the theater. Marlene was on fire and I wasn't about to put it out. We had a night of wild sex and I will never forget that birthday weekend. Marlene knew how to use her sensuality on me or any other man who crossed her path. Sex was her weapon.

The holiday season was rapidly approaching, our counseling was moving forward with no real breakthroughs and my morning bible reading wasn't being done as consistently as I had planned. I did mention Marlene's imaginary sister to Dr. Snyder and he said that topic hadn't come up during his sessions with Marlene. He said that was a sensitive area in her life and it's best that information be disclosed during her therapy. I wasn't doing well with remembering my dreams for analysis. Two dreams did have the doctor's attention. One was a recurring dream I had from my childhood. It involved walking down a long dark hallway in an apartment, but never reaching the door. The other dream was more recent. I was working at a temporary location across the street from our permanent office building. Dr. Snyder felt they were significant and dealt with my fear of separation from family, my children and my job. The long hallway may have signified an unfinished journey. I started having more difficulty remembering and writing down my dreams after sharing my last two with Dr. Snyder. He was great at not making me feel guilty and he appreciated my honesty. He advised me that he felt Marlene was holding back and not completely comfortable sharing more. I told him she was extremely private and most of the information I knew about her came from third parties. I added that she insisted on knowing everything about me. The doctor said it's an indication that she was hiding information. Sadly, after that session, I had an emergency meeting with Dr. Snyder.

Marlene was still working with the clients that had the toddler. Although I considered her to be a babysitter, she liked the stability. Working with elderly, terminally ill patients was very unstable and most engagements didn't last more than a month or two. One day, I left work and arrived home at noon, something I never did, to retrieve a folder I was working on over the weekend. When I entered the house, I was shocked to find the two-year-old baby at the top of the second floor staircase crying. He was attempting to walk down the steps. I quickly rushed upstairs and grabbed the child before he fell. I was appalled that Marlene would leave the baby alone and who knew for how long. If that little boy were injured in a fall or for any other reason, Marlene, the placement agency and anyone else the parents felt were liable, would be sued to the fullest extent of the law.

I heard Marlene coming through the front door. When she saw me she asked, "Why are you home so early?"

"You should be glad I came home when I did. The baby was about to fall down the stairs and I had to run up to grab him. Why would you leave a baby alone? I've been here for nearly a half hour!"

"The child was asleep when I left and I was coming right back!"

"Right back? How could you even consider leaving at all? That was irresponsible and totally asinine."

Marlene suddenly exploded. She rushed towards, grabbed my neck, and attempted to choke me. I pulled her hands from my throat and wrestled her to the floor. She scratched my hand and face as she struggled to get away from my hold. Besides her throwing that beer mug at me, this was the first time it became physical and violence accompanied an argument. It was horrible and the only reason she stopped fighting was because she heard the baby crying. I let her up as she ran to comfort the child. I left the house and quickly drove away. Thoughts were racing through my mind and I didn't know what to think. I couldn't go back to work because I was bleeding and had scratches on my nose and hand. I stopped at a drug store to buy Neosporin, and a styptic pencil which barbers use to stop the bleeding from razor cuts. The cuts weren't too deep and I was able to stop the bleeding. My next step was to get in touch with Dr. Snyder; he gave all of his clients a hot line number in case of an emergency. I used it and he returned my call in five minutes. Still upset, I told him what happened and he agreed to meet me at five that evening. In the meantime, I checked into a Holiday Inn, attempting to calm myself and gather my thoughts. We had just enjoyed Thanksgiving dinner at her parent's house and she was beginning her plans for her annual Christmas party. She wanted to invite some people from my office and I told her that wasn't a good idea. I explained, in my position, we had to invite the entire management staff so it doesn't show preferential treatment.

"I should be able to invite anyone I want. It's my party."

"Marlene, it wouldn't be politically correct."

In an effort to change the subject, I mentioned that I was looking forward to meeting her sister. Reminding her that she said Alice would be visiting during the holidays.

"She's coming to your fabulous Christmas party right?"

Her curt replied was, "I don't know what she's doing."

I was being clever and she didn't appreciate it.

I met with Dr. Snyder for more than an hour and he told me Marlene called as well. She told him that she was tired of my sarcastic remarks. She told him his therapy wasn't working and she would no longer participate in the bi-weekly sessions. Then the doctor began his most frank assessment about Marlene and our marriage.

He said, "A narcissist is two persons in one; a true self and a false self. The true self is insecure and imperfect, most likely hiding behavior she feels unacceptable to you or anyone else. Sometimes the lies are so deep in their subconscious, they aren't aware of the lies. There's nothing a narcissist won't do to keep this emotionally weak person from her world. Behind the mask of the ultra-confident false self lies a low self-esteem person who is vulnerable to the slightest criticism. The true self is virtually non-existent and has no role in the conscious life of a narcissist." I shook my head in disbelief, but he continued, "The false self is highly intelligent, virtuous and appears perfect in every way. Marlene truly believes that's who she is and people in her life must accept and admire the false self as her. However, the false self is a fraud and if she becomes enraged, she can cut a person out of her life with no regrets. If someone exposes the false self as a fraud, it would constitute an act of ultimate betrayal."

"So when I criticize her behavior in any way, I'm pouring fuel on the fire?"

"Correct."

I was numb from head to toe and finally, the doctor gave me a glimmer of hope. "Marlene can be helped, but it's extremely important that she continues her therapy. I don't feel the false self has completely suppressed or eliminated the true self, but she feels she deserves a better, painless and more considerate treatment from you and the people she let's into her world." Finally he said, "James, I know you love your wife and she has strong feelings for you. You must encourage her to keep an open mind about continuing her therapy. Recovery from narcissistic personality disorder will take time. Stay motivated to help Marlene and remind yourself the goal is to repair a damaged relationship and have a happy life with your wife."

I decided to spend the night at the hotel and hoped Marlene would calm down enough to talk the next day. I arrived at the office early and changed into the extra set of clothes I kept there. At noon, I received a call from the reservation clerk at the Portofino Hotel & Marina in Redondo Beach. She told me my wife reserved a room and I could go in any time to pick up my key. I was feeling good after that call, figuring that Marlene wanted to make up with me at a nice quiet resort over the weekend. It was a slow workday for a Friday so I left early. I wanted to have a fabulous weekend with my wife; I was invested in fixing our marriage, but I still needed guidance. The resort was minutes from King Harbor Marina and the Redondo Beach Pier. I picked up my key at the front desk and went straight to the room. When I opened the door, I saw my large storage chest on the floor and my two travel suitcases on the king size bed. Looking in the closet, I found more of my clothes hanging neatly, but no sign of Marlene's things. I began to have a feeling of despair when I saw a letter on the dresser.

The letter read, "Since you always leave our home when we have an argument, I assumed you wanted to have a new place to live. Have a good life!"

Once again, I was devastated. I asked God why this was happening to me and I heard His answer. He was preparing me for the adversity I was about to experience in my life.

The next ten days in that hotel room proved to be a spiritual awakening for me. I removed the luggage from the bed and laid there for several minutes thinking about how much more adversity I could possibly take in my life. I felt that I'd reached my limit emotionally and any more bad news would be overkill. I glanced at the brown clock on the bedside table, which read five thirty. I turned on the radio, leaned back and listened. I preferred R&B, Oldies, and Jazz. However, the radio was set to a station I wasn't familiar with. It was a Christian format that aired programs featuring nationally recognized spiritual leaders. All weekend, the station was promoting a new series of daily programs by Dr. David Jeremiah called *Facing the Giants in Your Life*. For the rest of the weekend, the station was concluding a series on the *Two Women in the Book of Proverbs*. At seven each night, I listened as the minster explained that each woman lived her life viewing God's plan completely different. A Man selecting the right life companion can mean the difference between heaven and hell. The women are described as the Clamorous Woman or

Dame Folly, which was a disrespectful, offensive and promiscuous woman who was looking for trouble. Conversely, the Virtuous Woman or Lady Wisdom was a faithful counselor and companion. She was a God-fearing woman who followed God's divine purpose for her life. Proverbs 31:12 states, "She does him good and does no harm all the days of her life." While Proverbs 21:19 describes the Clamorous Woman saying "It is better to live in a desert land than with a quarrelsome and fretful woman." Chapters five through nine gave warnings to men who are naturally vulnerable to sexual temptation that can plunge their lives into the depth of destruction. Chapter thirty-one speaks to the successful husband being supported and uplifted by his successful, Virtuous Wife. God was speaking to me in a powerful way that weekend and I couldn't wait to begin listening to *Facing the Giants in Your Life* series.

It became obvious that God wanted me to be diligent and consistent with my bible reading and I used that quiet time in the hotel to do just that. I read that He uses adversity in the life of a believer to bring that person closer to Him and His word. However, God limits the scope of the adversity and He provides a way to escape. I was learning that the dark moments in our lives will last only as long as it takes for God to accomplish His purpose in our lives.

All week I was diligent in learning. My week in the hotel room proved that I was not as alone as I thought I was. Marlene meant it as a form of punishment, but God meant it for good. I can't imagine how I would have survived that week filled with negative and hateful thoughts about my wife. I interpreted the Two Women in Proverbs lesson as two women living inside Marlene and that she had an opportunity to select the path to become the Virtuous Woman with prayer and God's help.

Monday was Christmas Eve and we were closing the office at noon. I knew God was preparing me for any adversity going forward in my life, however, the prospects of spending the Christmas holiday in that empty hotel room was depressing. Christmas was my favorite holiday and I had purchased Christmas gifts for my family back East as well as Marlene and the kids on Black Friday. I was sitting in Jeff Silver's office when the receptionist told me I had a call.

I picked up the phone and said, "This is James."

I heard Billy's voice, "Hi Pop, Merry Christmas."

"Merry Christmas to you. How long have you been home?"

He told me he went home for winter break and had been there for a week or so. He continued saying they had Christmas gifts for me and he wanted to know if he could stop by the hotel. I told him I would be there at one today. That was good because I was wondering how I was going to get their gifts to them. I discovered that Marlene did have her annual Christmas party Saturday night and invited people from my job. However, only one person from the office showed up and when he asked about me, Marlene told him I had an emergency earlier that day and I would probably miss the party. Billy arrived shortly after one and he looked great. We hugged and said how much we missed each other. He said his mother told him we had a big argument, but she didn't go into details. Billy stayed for over an hour and we talked about his adjustment to college life and the football season. It was a rebuilding year so the team finished with a losing record. He did win the starting tailback position and he broke the school's record for the total rushing yardage gained by a freshman. We exchanged gifts and he said he would call me the next day to wish me a Merry Christmas. We both got choked up, hugged again and said goodbye.

I looked around and thought about what my life had transitioned into and realized I had to transition out of that state. I ordered room service for lunch, turned on the radio, and listened to the Christian and gospel Christmas music that was permeating my soul. I was feeling down so I opened my bible to Proverbs and discovered a verse that would become one of my favorites. Proverbs 3:5-6 read, "Trust in the Lord with all your heart and lean not on your own understanding; in all ways acknowledge Him, and He will direct your path." At three thirty, I received a call from Marlene. She said she wanted me back home and she was sending Billy to help me with my luggage and the storage chest.

When Billy and I arrived home, Marlene greeted me with a brief hug and said she was working on Christmas dinner so she wouldn't have to deal with it on Christmas day. It was good to be home, but the atmosphere was strained. Marlene was pleasant but reserved and I got the feeling Billy had a lot to do with her inviting me back. By Christmas morning, she was back to normal as we opened gifts. I got Billy a Wilson A2000 pro model baseball glove. Another reason he chose Oregon State was the dual scholarship they gave him for football and baseball. He played both sports well, but football was his passion. Sarah's Dad gave her everything an eight-year-old girl would ever want or need, so it was always difficult to shop for her. That year, Marlene told him Sarah didn't want a doll, knowing that I had already purchased the new Harley Davidson Barbie doll for her and she loved it.

Marlene was a woman who had everything as well, so before I went shopping, I simply asked her to give me a list of five things she might want for Christmas. One of the items was a new watch. So I got her a Cartier Tank Solo watch and a Fendi handbag. Her reaction, as she opened her gifts, assured me I was back in her good graces. I did pretty well myself. She surprised me with a card that had a thousand dollars inside, which was her largest payment to date, towards the ten thousand credit card debt. As well, I found out that she purchased my expense birthday gift, the Versace leather suit on that maxed out gold card. Last summer when things were going well and we were seeing our therapist, I asked Marlene if she wanted to trade in her six-year-old BMW. That was the last car Lawrence purchased for her, other than the car he tried to give her two Christmas's ago. So I purchased a two-year-old, convertible Mercedes Benz. She loved the car. The kids got me a sweater vest and leather driving gloves that matched my leather suit. It truly was a lovely Christmas and dinner was great as usual. Between Christmas and New Years, Marlene took off work to be with Billy and Sarah and I took a couple of days to myself as well. Marlene was concerned because Sarah didn't feel well all week. She was having back and stomach pain. We decided to stay home New Years Eve for the first time since we'd been together because Sarah wasn't feeling any better. Her Dad was away for the holidays and wasn't expected back until the second of January, which was when he found out about Sarah's illness. This was the beginning of a series of events that I didn't anticipate. Nevertheless, it changed our lives forever.

Chapter 7

The Perfect Storm

A Perfect Storm is defined as a detrimental or calamitous situation or series of events arising from the powerful combined effects of a unique set of circumstances. I've been told that when you make the decision to get closer to God and His word, is when Satan starts to get busy disrupting your life.

Sarah was a little better but her dad insisted that Marlene take her to her pediatrician for a checkup. Marlene said ever since their daughter was born with a mild congenital heart defect, Lawrence has been overly cautious with Sarah's health, which explained why they didn't let her participate in any strenuous activities. It wasn't obvious that she had any health issues when observing her running around in the backyard playing with her big brother. The doctor stated that if the pain persisted, he would refer her to a cardiologist as a precaution. Marlene seemed unfazed. She said Sarah was a tough kid and she'd be all right.

Matters on the job were still unsettled. Due to a national recession that hit the last two quarters ending in December, the San Francisco market didn't meet their third or fourth quarter goals. Further, J.R. called me in early December advising me that the board was starting to put pressure on him to consider making changes. He asked me to send him my analysis for Plan C that I prepared but didn't present, last June, at the mid-year corporate meeting. Plan C was the most risky option we considered, as that plan would close the San Francisco operation. Knowing that the chairman of the board wasn't enthusiastic about the strategy we presented and the fact that the revenue goals presented weren't met was problematic. J.R. candidly informed me that Jeff and the San Francisco staff would only have the first quarter to show signs that things were improving. However, first quarters are traditionally slow in media advertising, so the prospects of that happening were slim.

The third element of that impending storm was the women who were terminated three years prior. I received a call from our L.A. corporate attorney, Howard Miles. He informed me that a lawyer who was considering representing two of the women, wanted to schedule a mediation meeting. Howard told me that several lawyers had turned down the case, but this was a young, hungry lawyer looking for some business. He said I didn't have to attend the meeting, but it would be good to have me there. I replied, "I'll be there!" The meeting was scheduled three weeks later. Attorney Miles and I agreed to meet one week prior to prepare.

That evening, I told Marlene about the pending mediation hearing and her only response was, "That's still going on?"

"Yes, it is." That was the end of the discussion.

I inquired about Sarah and she said her daughter had a good day. I was concerned about her nonchalant attitude, but that was probably how she dealt with stress. I knew she loved Sarah.

Our marriage continued without many highs or lows and I made sure not to hit any of Marlene's hot buttons, but sometimes, it was like walking on egg shells. Marlene refused to return to therapy, which disappointed Dr. Snyder and I, but she agreed to start attending Wednesday bible study at least twice a month. I shared the spiritual revelation I experienced in that hotel room with her. I was careful to emphasize the positive messages and avoided the Evil Woman described in the Book of Proverbs. I spoke about the Virtuous Woman highlighted in Proverbs 31 and how Marlene had many of her qualities. Marlene knew the bible well and I'm sure she was familiar with both women described in that book. One Sunday sermon was on marriage and the pastor said the key to any successful relationship was to "Forgive as Christ forgave us." His point was if or when your spouse hurts you, you must learn to forgive. It's a difficult task, but I was willing to try in an attempt to save our marriage.

Mediation day arrived and we met at the attorney's office. I was dressed in a blue, pinstriped business suit to make sure that I looked successful, but surprisingly, it was a low budget facility. The women, who I hadn't seen in over three years, looked the same and ineffective. My attorney introduced himself first, then me.

Their lawyer was taken aback and said, "I thought you were another attorney. Hello Mr. Fairchild."

"Good morning."

During the entire two-hour meeting, my former employees may have glanced in my direction two or three times and at its conclusion, walked out of the office without looking back. My attorney, Miles, covered every detail of the case and placed emphasis on the fact that the federal and state agencies that handled wrongful terminations and sexual harassment threw out the case years ago, stating the case had no merit. Miles used ninety minutes of the meeting and when he finished, their lawyer didn't have much to say. A week later, I received word that their attorney did not take the case, like the many attorneys before him. However, I did receive one last attempt of harassment by those women in our mailbox. The note read, "We won't stop until you don't have anything! Wife. Job. Nothing! That is a promise." I never heard from them again, but their curse was planted.

It was mid-March and the first quarter was ending. The sales were better than expected, but it was too little and too late to effect corporate plans to shut down the San Francisco office. I received the dreadful call from J.R. to come to D.C. for a meeting. This time, I was the only one attending; Jeff Sliver was not asked to come. I arrived on a red eye from L.A. at eight that morning and went straight to the office for the meeting at nine. I was told it would be held in the corporate attorney's office, so the handwriting was on the wall. I realized that *I* was being fired! That would be the first time I'd been terminated so I didn't know what to expect. The conversation wasn't short because J.R. explained the decision and shared how he truly appreciated my service and the personal relationship we had.

"Since we're now operating in one city and hired a West Coast controller to handle the finances, there's no room in the budget to support your salary." He sighed before continuing, "Although you've been exonerated from all charges concerning those women, corporate is receiving at least one complaint a month about you. Frankly, the board, President Thompson and I are all tired of the calls." Attorney Miles drew up an agreement to settle both claims for a nuisance value of four thousand in order to close the file and avoid further costs and expenses in the matter. I was hurt and heartbroken. I gave five years of my life to help build a successful company and ending it like that was devastating. They gave me a six-month severance package with medical coverage for my biological children and me, which made it a little less difficult. J.R. closed the meeting by saying, "Take as much time as you need cleaning out your office and please feel free to use us as a reference."

I thanked him for the opportunity the company had given me and wished them continued success. I thought about the entire situation on the way to the hotel. I should have known that was coming because, as with my wife, there were a number of red flags.

I decided to spend a couple of days in D.C. I called Marlene and left a voicemail stating that I needed to speak with her as soon as possible. I called my ex-wife to tell her I was in town for a couple of days and asked if I could stop by to see the children that evening. The last call was to the property management company who was taking care of my dad's house. I told them I wanted to drop by their office and see the house. They said that I could come by the next day. When Marlene returned my call, I gave her the bad news.

She calmly replied, "James, we'll be okay and you'll find another job with less stress. I'm claiming that."

"What a wonderful message," I told her. "I love you."

"I know. I love you too."

Then Marlene hit me with terrible news. They had to take Sarah to the emergency room the previous night and she was scheduled to see a cardiologist that Friday.

"Oh my God. She'll be alright; God has her."

I only saw Marlene cry once since we met, so I could tell she was fighting back tears.

"James, I have to go," she replied as she hung up promptly.

On Tuesday night, I was on another flight back to L.A. When I got home, Marlene was sitting on the sofa with Sarah. Marlene called off from work because Sarah hadn't been to school all week. I was amazed to see how normal Sarah and Marlene looked.

"James, you look awful. Did you get any sleep while you were away?"

"No, not really."

"Go get some rest and we'll talk later."

I was exhausted. I slept for five hours and woke up dazed not knowing where I was. Reality hit me moments later when I realized I was at home, my stepdaughter was very sick and I didn't have a job. Marlene was in the kitchen finishing preparations for dinner. We didn't have much of an appetite, but we ate quickly and were ready to have our conversation.

I told Marlene about how hurt and hopeless I felt when J.R. fired me. I was a loyal, dedicated employee of the company who made many personal sacrifices for its good. I assured her that our finances would be secure for several months because of the severance pay, but I wanted to start my search for a new job next week. Marlene listened quietly and made one or two comments of support. Then it was her turn to vent. She began by telling me that over the last few weeks, she noticed Sarah's breathing became rapid, had a loss of energy, wasn't eating well and losing weight. On Sunday, she and Lawrence noticed a slight blue tint to Sarah's skin tone and swelling of her ankles; that's when they rushed her to the hospital. I asked why she didn't take her to see a doctor earlier when she first noticed the changes in her daughter's health. The look on her face told me I was being critical and to back off. I didn't ask another question after that. Tests were taken at the hospital and they would go over the results on Friday with the cardiologist. Marlene paused for a minute and then began the most honest look into her mind and heart I'd experienced.

"James, you know I pray very well and I'm trying to be more faithful everyday. I committed to attend bible study with you and my going to church has become consistent and then this happens. My daughter is extremely ill and Lawrence told me that Sarah doesn't have health coverage because of her pre-condition. He's been paying her medical bills out-of-pocket and now you lost your job." She took a deep breath. "What is God telling me?" She was asking a rhetorical question that needed no response from me. She continued, "When we got baptized and I asked God to forgive me for the sins of my past, I felt a sense of freedom that was unbelievable. But now I can see that God didn't forgive me and that Lawrence and I are being punished with her illness."

"Marlene, you know God doesn't work like that."

"Do I?"

Marlene didn't go into details about her sins or Lawrence's past, but I imagined they were pretty deep and serious. It caused me to think back to the circumstances surrounding the death of Lawrence's first wife. I wasn't about to ask any questions, but most likely, that was because I didn't want to know. Marlene began talking about her childhood and being raised in a Christian home. She said she had seen and experienced many things that contradict God's word, which caused her to lose her faith at times. She thought her baptism would put her back on the right track with her faithfulness, but she felt she was wrong in her opinion. Still learning as a Christian, I didn't have any answers for my wife who was hurting and needed help from the Lord. I suggested that she schedule a meeting with our pastor and she replied, "I'll think about it."

I was happy she would consider it without immediately turning the idea down. Marlene was conflicted and the events of her past were coming back to haunt her. Again, I felt hopeless and needed guidance myself. At the next Bible study, I planned to speak with the pastor. Hopefully at that time, Marlene would take advantage of the opportunity to express her feelings. Of course, that was wishful thinking on my part because Satan was getting busy and Bible study was cancelled that week.

Only the parents were allowed to attend the meeting with the cardiologist and Sarah sat with the nurse while the details of her condition were discussed with Marlene and Lawrence. The results of the electrocardiogram and MRI detected an abnormal heart sound or murmur. I discovered that Sarah had been taking medication for years, but her condition had gotten worse. The heart specialist had to determine what course of action should be taken based upon her parent's desires and her diagnosis. It could be a medical procedure that would help improve her condition or major heart surgery. Sarah was diagnosed to have aortic valve disease and the doctor recommended surgery as the best way to go. The specialist felt Sarah's valve could be repaired and her parents agreed to schedule the surgery for the following Friday. I received the news when Marlene returned from the doctor's appointment and that was the second time I saw her cry. Sarah spent the weekend with her father.

I learned in graduate school to always have a résumé prepared and I only had to insert minor updates to have mine ready for distribution. I called Jeff while Marlene was out and told him I wanted to come to the office Saturday morning to retrieve my things. When I arrived, he came out of his office to greet me.

"James, I'm sorry about this. Everyone here is really down about the situation. If you need anything from me, you know how to reach me. You're the reason I'm here."

"Thank you. I'll leave my keys in my office–I mean, in my former office," I said dejectedly.

"Take your time," he added, walking away.

I didn't realize how much stuff I had until it was time to move. It took me three trips to finish moving from my Ascending Media Group office to my home. I was ready to turn the page and begin my job search. I began exploring the employment section in the Sunday L.A. Times. I found two positions that were interesting and slipped my updated résumé into large stamped envelopes and placed them in the corner mailbox. Monday morning's game plan was to call the major media and financial institutions in the Metro L.A. area to get contact information regarding human resources at each company. However, before I could get started, I received a call from J.R. He informed me that a media company based in Chicago was looking for a media executive with my background, so he referred them to me. He gave me the name and phone number of the managing partner, but said I should wait for him to call me later in the day because he was traveling. I thanked him for the referral and thanked God for opening another door. Positions like mine were difficult to secure and are usually found through referrals or word of mouth. It was a blessing that the lead came so quickly.

Thomas Simmons from the Simmons Group called me Monday evening.

"James, I've heard some great things about you," he said.

"Well, thank you."

"We have a newly created position I'd like to discuss with you. I'll be in San Francisco next week and I'd like to know if you'd be available to meet?"

"Yes, that sounds good. Any day after Monday will work for me."

"Let's meet next Tuesday at noon at The Fairmont Hotel."

"That's perfect. I look forward to meeting you there." I excitedly ran upstairs to tell Marlene the news. She was in Sarah's room making sure she was comfortable. Marlene and Lawrence made arrangements for Sarah to receive home schooling while she recovered from her pending surgery. Marlene resigned from her babysitting position so she could focus on her daughter and the recovery. Lawrence agreed to replace Marlene's lost income and supply anything she needed to care for their daughter. Despite the fact that Marlene's reaction to my possible job opportunity was tepid, Sarah's illness was bringing them closer together. I thought that was one positive outlook on the current circumstances.

"That sounds nice. If you get it, when would you start?"

"I don't know, but because of Sarah's illness I can ask to move the start date back."

"That won't be necessary. I'll be staying at the hospital while Sarah's there and only parents can stay with her for extended periods."

"Marlene, I want to be there for you. Just let me know so I can be up front about our situation when I meet with Mr. Simmons."

"I wouldn't mention anything about our situation or Sarah's illness."

"Okay then."

Billy flew in Thursday night so he could be with the family during his sister's operation. Sarah had to be at the hospital early Friday morning. The surgery was set to take place at ten and would last between four and six hours. Billy and I arrived an hour before Marlene's parents, two sisters and her brother. They were in the waiting area along with Lawrence and Marlene. I brought my Bible and *100 Prayers of Encouragement*, and read passages all morning. Two hours into the surgery, Lawrence came over to where I was sitting and sat down. I had brief conversations with him over the years so that was a surprise. Again, our talk was short but meaningful to me.

"I appreciate you bringing your Bible and how well you've treated my daughter. She's–she's very fond of you." Then I could see a different look in his eyes. He said something that was from his heart, "I don't know why this is happening to my baby girl, my angel. She's my heart and I don't know what I would do if anything happened to her. James, you're a good person. Continue to pray for her and please say a prayer for me." Lawrence got up and returned to his seat on the other side of the room before I could respond.

The operation lasted almost seven hours because there were some complications. However, the heart surgeon felt the operation was a success and Sarah's prognosis was excellent. He recommended that she stay in the hospital for ten days to two weeks so they could have hands-on observation during the initial stage of her recovery. Marlene's father said a prayer with the family before we returned home. Marlene and Lawrence stayed at the hospital.

Billy waited until he was assured Sarah was going to be fine before he returned to college on Saturday night. I used my time preparing for my interview with Mr. Simmons. The Simmons Group was a medium-sized advertising agency. It added two major accounts the first of the year. Those accounts were so large, it afforded the company an opportunity to expand its staff and create the new position I was pursuing. Thomas Simmons was much younger than I expected. He began his career as a fast track junior executive for J. Walter Thompson and reached the level of senior vice president for national advertising, when he decided to leave Thompson and start his own company seven years prior. His agency focused on brand building and business-to-business transactions. The position we were talking about was the newly created vice president of New Business Development and Acquisitions. He felt my experience in developing Ascending Media Group's West Coast business was just what he needed to grow his company. The interview went very well and we both felt it was a good match. Mr. Simmons ended our conversation by asking what type of compensation package I was looking for and he wanted to know my ending salary.

I gave him the number and he responded, "If I increase that by twenty percent do we have a deal?"

"Mr. Simmons, just put your offer in writing and we'll have a deal."

The next day, I received a FedEx package with a contract ready for my signature. The only issue was they wanted me to start in three weeks, so I had to discuss that date with Marlene before I signed the contract. The only time Marlene came home was to change clothes and get school assignments for Sarah. I had a brief conversation with her about the terms of the contract and the proposed start date. She seemed excited for me and said it wouldn't be a problem because Sarah should be home in two weeks.

Two incidences occurred while I was home alone. After ten days of Sarah's hospitalization, the postman delivered several days of mail. Marlene had placed a one-week hold on mail delivery since she would be spending the majority of her time at the hospital. The mail included credit card, department store and household bills I knew nothing about. The bills were in my name, so Marlene had to obtain the cards using my credit information. This was troubling but she must have been making the payments because I hadn't received any calls requesting payment. I was sure when she requested the hold on our mail delivery she didn't think Sarah would have to stay in the hospital so long. The next incident was regarding two repairmen that showed up one afternoon. They told me the woman who owned the house wanted them to inspect the air-conditioning and roof for possible repairs. I told them there must be some mistake because Lawrence Allen was the homeowner. They showed me the work order, which indicated a woman's name as the property owner. I was confused and both occurrences were concerning. When I was in therapy, it was determined that when I recognized an incident as being unusual I should address it. The problem in that case was timing. Marlene and Lawrence were dealing with a serious health issue. Credit card bills and rent payments would be the least of their concerns. I decided to keep the information to myself and wait until things were back to normal before I addressed the matter with Marlene.

It was time for me to leave for Chicago on Saturday afternoon. Marlene came home Saturday morning and told me she asked her friend, Larry Hill, to take me to the airport. Sarah was scheduled to come home on Tuesday and Marlene had a meeting with the cardiologist at noon. She stayed with me until eleven and it was hard to see her so emotional. She told me that she loved me and she was sorry for the hard times she put me through. At that point, her eyes welled with heavy tears and she started crying. I couldn't help but shed a few tears as well. I wrapped her in my arms and she sorrowfully returned the embraced for five minutes. While her head was pressed against my chest, she said she had to go and to call her when I arrived in Chicago. She looked up, gave me a quick kiss and added, "We're going to miss you." I didn't know what to say because all I could feel was heartbroken. Marlene's words sounded so final and it dawned on me that she may never move to Chicago with me.

Larry picked me up and drove me to LAX. Our conversation was enlightening and connected me to reality. I think he wanted me to understand some things about Lawrence and Marlene he thought I should know. Once again, he said he thought I was a great guy, especially for Marlene and the kids, but Lawrence was still in love with her and would never free her from his control. Further, she knew too much about him and his insurance fraud. He had major fires at his home and business over the years. With Marlene's help and lies supporting that both fires were accidental, he received significant settlements. Lawrence had great contacts with contractors and was able to rebuild his house and business at a fraction of the replacement cost his insurance company paid, so he was able to pocket the difference and give Marlene some of the money.

"Rachel and I love Marlene, but her greatest weakness is her love of money and Lawrence uses that weakness to his advantage every chance he gets," Larry admitted.

"Larry, why are you telling me this now?"

"I just felt it was information you needed to know James," he said as he reached over and patted my shoulder. "Besides, Marlene told us you hate surprises."

I thanked Larry for the ride to the airport and the information he shared. We hugged and said goodbye. As I waited to board, I thought about Larry's suggestion. With me being in another state, Lawrence was back in full control of Marlene. Money was like a trail of breadcrumbs to her dishonest way of life and it fed her soul what she craved. Her spiritual upbringing never quite made it to her core, which allowed her to deteriorate even faster than she knew.

The Allure of a Predator

Chapter 8

The Transition

My new company made arrangements for me to live in their corporate apartment for my first six months in Chicago. In the past, I never stayed in the Windy City more than a few days on business trips, but I enjoyed the town. The Lakeshore Apartments sat atop of a six-acre public park near the city's central business district. It was one of the most popular areas to live because of the shopping, dining, cultural and entertainment opportunities right in the Lakeshore East neighborhood. The apartment was beautifully furnished with dark hardwood floors throughout. The kitchen had custom mahogany cabinets, granite countertops and stainless steel appliances. I told Mr. Simmons, "It's going to be difficult to leave this place when my six-month stay ends." He laughed in agreement. The company's office was located in the central business district as well, which made it easy to walk to work everyday if the Chicago winter weather permitted.

I'd been calling Marlene every day to check on Sarah's recovery and her adjustment to me being away. "Sarah's progressing, which is great. I can tell her health crisis has changed Lawrence's attitude and overall demeanor." She paused before she continued again, "He's kinder and gentler now."

I was happy to hear that, but I wondered if Lawrence's change was due to me being absent.

"I miss having you home." She named one of her sex toys after me and said, "We're developing a nice relationship, but I miss the real thing." I knew she was just trying to tease me. Regardless, I was blushing at the thought.

"Marlene, everyone is looking forward to meeting you because I talk about you so much."

"What do you tell them?"

"I brag about what a great mother and wife you are. And that you're gorgeous."

She laughed and said, "You're still so silly, even in Chicago."

"I know. What can I say? I guess I'm consistent," I replied.

The Simmons Group held their anniversary party every November, which was our wedding anniversary as well. Marlene and I never really celebrated ours, but since she was coming to Chicago for the first time to attend the company's party, we agreed to combine both anniversaries and have a spectacular celebration and reunion together. I could tell Marlene was excited and looking forward to the trip, but Sarah's health was the priority and that would be the only reason she wouldn't come to Chicago. I prayed every night for God's healing power to bless my stepdaughter.

Since my position was recently created, I had a lot of input regarding my responsibilities and duties. My major responsibilities included maintaining the company's existing accounts within the United States and Canada. In addition, I had to implement marketing and sales strategies that involved forecasting and attaining company goals. My experience with Ascending Media Group and working closely with Jeff Silver made me confident that I was well prepared to excel in my new position. The acquisition duties of my job were not immediate and Mr. Simmons felt his growth plan for the company was two or three years away. I enjoyed working with Mr. Simmons and the staff was excellent. After one month on the job, I knew I made the right choice.

Sarah was on the road to recovery and she was ahead of the doctor's schedule. She was getting stronger every day and Marlene said her energy level was rapidly increasing, but she had to make sure Sarah wasn't trying to do too much. Lawrence agreed to take care of her while Marlene came to Chicago. Marlene planned to arrive the day before the company's anniversary event and stay for ten days. This would allow us to celebrate our wedding anniversary together in Chi-Town.

That week flew by and I was excited to pick my wife up from the airport. She was dressed in a gold Nike sweat suit with matching running shoes. She looked well rested, which was completely different from her appearance when she was looking after Sarah. She genuinely seemed happy to see me.

She ran and jumped into my arms announcing cheerfully, "I missed you so much!"

"I really missed you too. And you look great, as always."

Marlene had three pieces of luggage in addition to her carry on bag. It seemed as though she brought enough clothes to stay for the month. I wondered if she was planning on it.

Marlene was impressed when she entered my corporate apartment. "I thought your apartment in L.A. was nice, but it doesn't compare to this place." Exploring the space, she continued, "Everything in this place is fabulous! I love the furniture, amenities, the artwork, the color scheme, everything."

Yeah, it's great. The building has an indoor pool and a fully equipped workout facility too.

"Wow, I'm impressed. I just might consider moving here."

"What do you mean you *just might consider moving here?*"

She quickly replied, "Relax James, I'm kidding."

I really didn't know if she was. We enjoyed dinner at a neighborhood Chinese restaurant and spent the rest of the night making up for lost time. The company anniversary party was held in the Ritz-Carlton Grand Ballroom. Company employees and their significant others, clients and the top power players and celebrities of Chicago were invited. Again, Marlene was beautiful. I looked down at her Gucci, Jaguar print heels. My gaze lifted to her black Armani Collezioni sheer dress, her 18k gold necklace and diamond earrings.

Mr. Simmons and his wife were gracious and complimented us by saying we were an elegant couple. I was wearing a Hugo Boss Aikin Hollo trim fit wool tuxedo with a black silk tie and Bruno Magli oxford shoes. At that point, I was trying to keep up with Marlene. It was a wonderful event and Mr. Simmons made a special introduction of Marlene and me to the star-studded crowd. I was now on an elevated level. Mr. Simmons and Marlene Fairchild put me there.

During Marlene's stay in Chicago, she visited me at the office and met the staff in a less formal setting. Everyone seemed to like her. She went shopping on Michigan Ave, although she had a spending limit, and enjoyed the park and restaurants in my neighborhood. We celebrated our anniversary at Hyde Park Steakhouse and I presented her with two-dozen roses. It was the wonderful honeymoon we never experienced. To my surprise, we received the Hawaii vacation promised by Ascending Media Group, which was to serve as a replacement for our aborted honeymoon at Lake Tahoe. However, that trip was scheduled during one of the rough patches in our marriage and Marlene didn't agree to go until the night before the flight. Her behavior dampened my spirit, so it wasn't a memorable experience. It reminded me of the Lake Tahoe disaster. If judged by our lovemaking and overall positive interaction, we could convince anyone that we were madly in love and would be together forever. However, this was the last time we had such a loving and enjoyable time as a couple.

The next time I saw my wife and stepchildren was on Christmas. It was the first time in years that Marlene didn't have her annual party. She said Sarah's medical condition and expenses were the primary reason for the cancellation of the party, but the real reason was Lawrence's refusal to underwrite Marlene's signature event. Due to my involvement with completing end of year projects and first quarter projections, I could only stay in California for three days and had to leave the day after Christmas. Marlene appeared to go out of her way to be on her best behavior because she knew Christmas was my favorite holiday. It was great to see Billy and Sarah's progress. All three days were family oriented, so Marlene and I had little time together. Regardless, it was nice to spend quality time with loved ones. On the drive to the airport, Marlene made a disturbing statement that confirmed that she still had serious issues she had yet to address.

She said, "James, I forgot to tell you my sister Alice, Billy's mom, is coming to visit and she's taking me and the kids to Lake Tahoe." Before I could respond she continued, "She wants us to go skiing and she made special arrangements for Sarah's care while the rest of us are on the slopes." I was baffled; I didn't know what to say.

On the flight back to Chicago, I tried to determine what Marlene was up to and who was taking my family on a vacation. Marlene called me at midnight on New Years Eve to wish me a happy New Year, but not wanting to be alone on New Years Eve, I decided to go to one of the many parties I was invited to. More importantly, before going to the party, I attended a special New Year's Eve service at the church I joined a month earlier. The next day, I spoke with Marlene and she was happy to hear I went out. She said everyone was having a good time. I was tempted to ask if I could speak with her sister, but I didn't want to hear another lie.

There was only one person who probably knew the truth, so a couple of days later, I called Larry. After a bit of small talk, I got to the reason for my call.

"Larry, I appreciated our candid conversation and the information you shared when I was leaving for my new position in Chicago. What I'd like to know is if you have any idea who took my family on the Tahoe trip?"

"Is that all?" he asked with a chuckle as if I were clueless. "It was her ex-husband Lawrence," he replied. "Since Sarah's illness and your leaving, Marlene and Lawrence have gotten closer. But she's only allowing it to get the extra money he's giving her."

"What about the guy who played for the Raiders; her former boyfriend? Does he help financially?"

"You're talking about Jo Jo Moore?"

"Yeah, I guess so."

"Marlene and Jo Jo had a thing after she divorced Lawrence, but it didn't last. After he retired from football, he didn't have any real skills and lost all his money on bad business investments. Marlene kept him around as a gofer and a backup if she needed help doing something physical."

"Really?"

"Of course. He's the person who helped her move your things to that hotel when you guys separated a while back."

I always wondered how she moved my things, but I figured it was Lawrence, Billy or even Larry. Again, Larry was helpful and I thanked him for his time.

It was Super Bowl Sunday when I received a call from Marlene. I figured she was going to tell me about her annual party at Larry and Rachel's house. But when I heard her voice, I knew something was terribly wrong.

"Is Sarah alright?"

"There's been a horrible accident! Lawrence is in the hospital with third degree burns over most of his body!" she said with a trembling voice.

"What happened?" I asked.

"The police told me there was a major explosion at his auto shop and he was trapped in there. They were surprised he found a way out, but he's in critical condition and on life support."

"Oh my God. What do you need me to do?"

She replied, "I need you home! I need you now!"

"I'll call you back when I find a flight."

I hung up the phone and called Mr. Simmons to tell him about the emergency. He said, "Go to your family. We'll take care of business here." I was on a flight back to L.A. that evening. I met Marlene at the hospital on Monday morning and saw the severity of Lawrence's condition. He suffered burns from head to toe and his chances for recovery looked nonexistent. It was a matter of time before they would take him off life support. Lawrence's family, two sisters and brother, arrived from Dallas that afternoon and that's when the real drama began.

I could tell that Lawrence's sisters didn't like Marlene because they could hardly look at her. Five minutes after they arrived at the hospital, Marlene told me we should leave. Marlene admitted that his sisters always blamed her for the problems Lawrence had in his first marriage. They were revolted at how swiftly she and Lawrence were married after her death.

"Did they feel you had anything to do with his wife's death?"

She looked away for a moment and then replied, "They didn't go *that* far, but his former wife's family made the accusations. Those claims were mainly directed towards Lawrence." I didn't know if Marlene was being honest. Perhaps the tragedy would provide the breakthrough needed for her to confront the dishonesty and lies in her past.

The next morning, Marlene wanted me to go to the DMV and L.A. County Auditor's office to research Lawrence's real estate holdings and the vehicles he owned. What I discovered was a huge surprise to Marlene and I. Over the past two years, Lawrence was liquidating most of his assets. I found out that he only owned two vehicles, his personal BMW and his company van. In regards to property, he owned the auto repair business property and his home, which had a mortgage because he recently refinanced it.

Marlene laughed nervously and said, "There must be some mistake. You must have missed some records."

"I'm surprised too. I asked the clerk if she had any idea where other records could be found. She told me I was at the right place and the information I found was correct."

Marlene looked shocked and said, "He drives four different cars and he owns over ten different properties!"

I replied, "Maybe at one time, but that's not the case now. The other cars were probably leased, loaners or just rentals. A woman at the DMV knew Lawrence and was surprised he was still around and in business since he was having severe financial problems a few years ago. Were you aware of that?"

"Of course not. And what that woman told you was nothing more than useless gossip."

It was clear that what I shared put Marlene in a solemn mood. She informed me that Lawrence's family had decided to take him off life support. He was pronounced dead at two the next morning.

Over the following three days, Marlene and his family argued over Lawrence's business and personal assets, including his insurance polices and will. It was determined that the executor of his limited estate was his older sister. Furthermore, due to the nature of his death, any insurance claims would have to be investigated. After the third day, I asked Marlene when they were going to stop fighting and make funeral arrangements for the poor man. But she wasn't sure. Lawrence was in financial distress; to my knowledge, there was only twenty thousand in cash and twelve thousand had to be used for his funeral and burial, due to the hold on his insurance allocation.

The funeral was finally scheduled for the following Friday and Marlene asked me to pay six hundred for a floral arrangement shaped as a horses head that would cover the entire casket. Lawrence loved horses and at some point, owned two or three. One of them was Sarah's, too. Owning horses was costly and with the discovery of his financial situation, I made the assumption that they were part of his liquidation process. The funeral service was held at an upscale facility and presided over by a funeral director, since Lawrence didn't have a church affiliation. The major problem, however, was Billy's omission from the program. He wasn't listed as a son, stepson, nephew or any family designation. He was humiliated by the omission and I was embarrassed for him. Marlene explained it away by blaming it on Lawrence's evil sisters trying to hurt her. I wasn't sure what to think. I returned to Chicago at the end of weekend.

Three months after Lawrence's death, the insurance investigation was concluded. The business claim was deemed fraudulent and denied. It was determined that Lawrence caused the explosion for insurance purposes. His prior claims involving the fires at his business and home were scrutinized too.

The family was informed that committing insurance fraud was a felony, but they wouldn't pursue criminal action against his estate, since Lawrence died in the explosion. The good news was his life insurance claim was paid because it was concluded that his death was accidental and it wasn't his intention to be killed in the explosion. Lawrence didn't have health insurance for Sarah because of her precondition and her medical expenses were astronomical. He needed money and cashing in on insurance claims was his mode of operation. This time, the results were deadly and had a major impact on Marlene's financial stability. Lawrence's sister was the beneficiary of his life insurance policy and it was stipulated in his will that Sarah would receive a twelve hundred monthly stipend until she turned twenty-one, then she would obtain a lump payment of two hundred and fifty thousand. Those terms couldn't support Marlene's lifestyle and the next month, she sent me a package filled with bills she could no longer pay. The bills added an additional fifteen hundred to my monthly expenses and affected the amount of money I was sending her every month. The six months of free rent at the corporate apartment ended, but because of my personal situation, Mr. Simmons extended my stay for sixty additional days. I admitted to Marlene that attempting to support two households would not be possible, especially because of the additional bills I didn't know of. She agreed to visit and look at places to live as well as hospitals for Sarah's care. It was becoming clear that if Lawrence was still living, he would have never let Marlene take Sarah to another state and I believe Marlene would have been okay with it.

I knew Marlene's second visit to Chicago would be her last. She was less than enthusiastic as she looked at potential places to live. There were beautiful homes and Chicago had a world-class hospital network but nothing satisfied her. One month later, I moved into a house that she thought was nice and she called me to say the timing wasn't right for her, so she wasn't coming. I didn't have the slightest idea what our future would bring, but I was sure I'd find out soon enough.

Chapter 9

Escape From Consumption

My marriage was in crisis. I felt it was cruel the way Marlene called on the day I was supposed to move in when she had no intentions to live there. The house was located in a suburb twenty-two miles from downtown. She knew I signed a one-year contract with an option to buy, which allowed us some flexibility to find something closer to the city. At that point, she should have told me she was having reservations and I would have found a place in the same neighborhood where the corporate apartment was located. The house was listed for nearly five hundred thousand dollars and I would be paying twenty five hundred per month. It was four bedrooms, three baths and a three thousand square foot Colonial style home that Marlene said she liked. It was a two-story custom-built brick house with a gourmet kitchen, oak cabinets, and a fireplace in the family room. The open staircase led to a beautiful master bedroom that included a Jacuzzi in the master bath. Frankly, it was a more exquisite home than our house in L.A. and equivalent to a million dollar property in California. I knew I'd be reminded every day that Marlene stood me up. I was infuriated.

During my bible study, I learned that when adversity happens, we become more vulnerable and we start doubting God's presence in our life. I was in pain emotionally and wondered why God let Marlene hurt me again. But adversity is God's way of making us stronger and drawing us closer to Him. How could I be lonely in that house if I had God and continued to read His word? Of course that's easier said than done, but my faith in the Lord got me through difficult trials. I realized God was always with me because my personal life didn't affect my performance at work. Mr. Simmons was supportive and said I was on a fast track to run my own media agency once they decided the timing was right to expand to another market.

More than six months passed before I heard from Marlene. I attempted to reach her a few times with no success and when I traveled to L.A. to meet with my tax attorney, I discovered she had moved without leaving a forwarding address. Obviously, she was moving on and didn't care if I knew where. I decided it was time to part ways formerly and protect myself from any additional financial harm she might cause since we were still married. My attorney said he would do some research to see if he could get an address for her and he would forward it to me. About two weeks later, he called with an address. A co-worker referred me to an excellent female divorce lawyer.

Our initial consultation went well but she confessed, "Mr. Fairchild, I know you feel your situation with your narcissistic wife is bad, but I've handled cases that were more abusive than yours. Fortunately, you're a financial person so you monitored your financial records better than most." We agreed that the sooner we served divorce papers to Marlene, the better. We hired a professional process server to hand-deliver the summons and the complaint to Marlene. The problem was when the server attempted to deliver the divorce papers to the address my tax attorney obtained; it was a UPS mailbox with a real street address. I didn't know what that meant, but I probably needed to hire the private investigator again. I was certain Mr. Carmichael would find her in no time, but my attorney suggested a public notice divorce for a missing spouse. First, I completed an Affidavit of Diligent Search, which my lawyer notarized. Then a Public Notice of Divorce was placed in the legal classified section of the Chicago Tribune. After the notice ran for a specified time limit, my divorce was granted on the grounds of a default by the absentee spouse.

I was free at last and ready to let go of the past when I received a call from Wells Fargo Bank of California. I took the call and was informed that I was behind three payments on the Mercedes Benz. I explained that the car was my former wife's vehicle and it was in her possession in L.A. They said the car was in my name and if I didn't make the payments, the car would be subject to repossession. I asked if I could have forty-eight hours to try to locate the car, which they agreed upon. Marlene was trying to be deceitful. The car payment was the only bill she didn't send to me. Since I was making payments on her other bills, she figured I would begin paying for the car too, but she was mistaken. She loved that car and I refused to

221

pay for it. I was going to track down Marlene if it was the last thing I did! I called the private investigator and explained my dilemma. Carmichael called back in two hours with her home address and the doctor's office where she was now working.

"Thank you for your help, Earl. Can you just send the invoice to my home address?"

"Don't worry about it James; there's no charge. I *never* trusted that woman."

I called Wells Fargo and they repossessed the car by the end of the business day. I hadn't heard from Marlene in over nine months, so to hear her voice threw me off when she called me early the next morning at my office. No small talk was necessary; she got straight to the point.

"James, what happened to the car?" She used the sweet, innocent voice she typically used to get what she wanted.

I curtly replied, "The bank called and said you were three payments in arrears. They said they needed a payment today or the car would be repossessed. I told them I didn't have the payment and *you* had the car. So I guess the only way I'd finally hear from you after all these months of silence is when something you love is taken from you. They took the car."

I figured she didn't appreciate my tone or attitude because she hung up without saying goodbye. An attorney representing Marlene called later that day asking if I would sign the vehicle over to Marlene if she assumed liability. I gave him my lawyer's number and told him to speak to her knowing that I already informed her of the situation after Marlene hung up. The attorneys came to an agreement that I signed. Wells Fargo Bank notified me the following week that

Marlene Fairchild paid the fourteen thousand in full. At the time, I didn't know how she pulled it off, but she was good at targeting victims and exploiting their weaknesses. Another negative aspect of my financial dealing was the car repossession on my credit report. My outstanding credit history would be tainted for many years to come and it was all due to the allure of a predator. I was sure if she hadn't found her next victim already, he was already within her sites.

As my story unfolded, that was the end of my relationship and communication with Marlene. I never saw her again. I thanked God every day for allowing me to escape from consumption. My professional life continued in a positive direction because I had clear focus and passion. The company added new accounts monthly and Mr. Simmons was ready to take the next step to grow his business. I prepared the analysis for the possible acquisition of a small advertising agency in Atlanta, Georgia. The company was a prime target for a friendly takeover because we could help them capitalized their operation. The owner was an older gentleman who had no interest in expansion at that stage of his career. He was simply looking to cash out to a company like the Simmons Group. The company had a small staff but they had an excellent record in the market. Mr. Simmons felt it was an ideal opportunity for me to lead a small but established company into our culture of growth and continued client satisfaction. I was ready for a new challenge.

The Allure of a Predator

Chapter 10

The Call

Ten years had passed since my divorce. I was remarried to a beautiful, southern Christian woman who I met at an UNCF event. We just had a child together, which was my third. My older son and daughter were now young adults. I was a Regional Vice President for the southern region, which included Atlanta, Charlotte, Nashville, and Birmingham. For the first time in a long time, I was enjoying both my professional and more importantly, my personal life. My new wife was a prayer warrior so I was covered from the crown of my head to the soles of my feet. My mother, Aunt Vera and my children all love her dearly. After my experience with Marlene, many of my family and friends didn't think I would walk down the aisle again and I had serious doubts myself. But Ann Marie swept me off my feet and the timing was right for both of us; it was God's time!

Ann Marie and baby Cliff were visiting her parents in Nashville when I received a call at home one evening. The gentleman introduced himself as Dr. Montgomery.

"Is this James Fairchild?"

"Yes, can I help you?"

"I hope you can. Do you know Marlene Montgomery, formerly Marlene Allen?" he asked.

I almost fell out of my chair and drop the phone at the same time. I hadn't heard that name uttered in more than ten years.

Regaining my composure I asked, "Who did you say you are?"

"I know this might seem strange; my name is Bernard Montgomery and I'm a doctor. I'm married to Marlene, but I just found out about you last week."

"Dr. Montgomery, my marriage to that woman was the lowest point in my life and if you don't mind, she is the last person I want to discuss with anyone."

He pleaded, "Would you please give me a few minutes of your time. I really have something important to share with you."

The man sounded so desperate I just couldn't hang up on him. "How can I help you?"

As he began speaking, my mouth fell agape. Marlene was still using her allure as a predator. What he shared with me over two conversations would make anyone sick to their stomach. He told me he hired a private investigator, which was how he got in touch with me. Marlene never told him she was married to anyone other than Lawrence Allen who supposedly died in a car accident and left her and her children over two million dollars in insurance settlements. He said they had one little boy and adopted a young girl.

"How are Sarah and Billy?"

"They're fine. Sarah is how I met Marlene. I was on the team of physicians who performed her heart surgery and I worked with her extensively after the operation. At first, it was a doctor-patient relationship but shortly after her husband's death, the relationship became more personal."

I wanted to ask how personal, but then I really didn't want to know. He asked me how long we were married and when I gave him the dates, he answered my question.

He gasped, "Oh my goodness. I'm so sorry. We began dating while you were still married to her."

At that point I was done. I said, "Dr. Montgomery, it seems like you have a lot more to tell me, but right now, I'm in a very strange place, emotionally. Let's stop for tonight. We can continue this conversation on Saturday."

"I understand. But Mr. Fairchild, this is the tip of the iceberg. I'm filing for divorce tomorrow so can I call at ten?"

"That's fine."

When I hung up the phone, I dropped my face into my hands. I wasn't able to process everything and I felt disgusted. She was preying upon this man as if she didn't learn anything or have remorse or compassion for her actions. I actually felt sorry for Dr. Montgomery. Marlene most likely targeted him before Lawrence died in that explosion and I wondered how she was pulling off that rich widow act. I would soon find out.

Ann Marie and my son weren't due home until Sunday, so I would be able to continue my conversation with Dr. Montgomery uninterrupted. My wife knew about Marlene and me. I explained that it was a difficult marriage without going into the

227

unpleasant details. When I told her that I received a call from Marlene's husband, it took her by surprise.

"What did he want? Is she ok?" she asked.

"I think he's having some marital problems and since I was married to her, he's seeking advice." I knew it was more than that, but I didn't want to burden her with such a negative situation. "I'll speak with him tomorrow morning, so Ann, please lift him up in your prayers."

"Of course."

Marlene's husband called exactly at ten that morning and he seemed eager to continue where we left off. He explained his urgency to file for divorce was due to an office fire that destroyed much of his business records. Marlene caused the fire after he confronted her about missing funds. As a part of his investigation, his lawyer suggested that he conduct an internal audit with an outside accounting firm. He told me that Marlene was his office manager and handled the practice's bookkeeping. Further, she had a close relationship with the accounting firm he was using, but he recently terminated their contract. The internal audit uncovered massive misappropriation of funds. His first reaction was that there must have been fraudulent activity by the accounting firm. However, the results of a more detailed discovery process found the culprit was his wife, Marlene. He fired his accounting firm because they were negligent in their duties for allowing such a significant fraud to take place. It was obvious to me that Marlene used her powers of manipulation to influence the company's accountant to look the other way.

I asked, "Can you disclose the amount of fraud?"

"Three million dollars over a five year period," he replied.

"Oh my Lord!"

"James, there's more."

"Somehow, I'm not surprised." He told me that the new accounting firm thought Marlene was embezzling funds prior to their marriage. They had been married for seven years but those records were incomplete. She had over a million dollars in credit card debt that she was paying with company funds. My math brought the total to four million dollars in misappropriation of funds.

"It's obvious my partners and I have a very successful medical practice, but no company can absorb such a significant loss in funds without suffering enormous financial hardship. Two of my partners had to take second mortgages on their homes and one is considering a lawsuit since it was my wife who committed the fraud. My practice and life is in shambles."

"Your situation is unbelievable and horrific, but I don't see how I can help you."

"My lawyer thinks you can," he replied.

"How so?"

"I'm attempting to have our marriage annulled because she married me under false pretences. She never indicated she was married to anyone other than Lawrence and when I confronted her about you, she said it wasn't a real marriage, but one out of convenience.

"What does *that* mean?" I asked.

He replied, "She said you were gay and needed to be married for professional and business reasons. The investigator said that was bogus based upon your three children and your current marital status."

Marlene was a professional predator who used her allure, lies, and manipulation to defraud men. All of the signs were there but I refused to respond to them appropriately. I allowed the situation to manifest in hopes that she would submit to God. I wanted her to get better and perhaps it was because I wanted my marriage to work.

Contrary to my Christian teaching, my pride and ego kicked in when I asked, "Why would she stay in a marriage of convenience if she wasn't getting anything out of it? She did some financial damage to me and it was sickening, but it was nowhere close to what she did to you. Your situation is beyond criminal! Did she tell you about our sexual activities?"

That was a rhetorical question and I asked it out of anger. I went on to tell him some of the activities without getting too graphic. After a brief pause he responded, "Yes, that sounds like things Marlene likes to do." Getting back on track, he said his attorney would like to schedule a deposition with me and he would fly me out to California. He added that he would pay for all of my expenses in addition to the fee I would charge.

"I don't require a fee. If you'll fly your lawyer to Atlanta, I'll do the deposition here."

"I have to discuss that with my attorney but I don't have any problem with those arrangements. Thank you for your time Mr. Fairchild. My attorney will call next week."

Marlene was unbelievable. She was married to a millionaire doctor and still felt compelled to steal his money. He said she bought Billy and Sarah new cars when they graduated from college and high school, respectively. Then she flew a female friend, who she met through me, all over the states on shopping sprees and vacations. I called Jada Jones, our mutual friend, with the news. She said Marlene did fly her and her daughter, who was the same age as Marlene's son, on all expenses paid vacations. She, like the doctor, thought Marlene's money came from her ex-husband's estate and life insurance policies.

"Marlene's new husband just found out about me and called to see if she did similar things to me. Then she had the nerve to tell him I was gay!"

Jada laughed and replied, "That's funny. She often told me about the things you guys did in bed. I'd get so uncomfortable and wonder why she was telling me those things."

Growing embarrassed, I quickly changed the subject, "When was the last time you spoke to her?"

"More than two years ago. I tried calling her several times but she never returned my calls."

"Yeah, I know. That's how she operates."

Dr. Montgomery's attorney called me on Tuesday morning and we scheduled the deposition to take place in two weeks; he said he would email me the location and time within forty-eight hours.

The Allure of a Predator

Chapter 11

The Deposition

Russell Washington, Dr. Montgomery's attorney, conducted a conference call with me prior to the deposition to explain the process and his objectives. His goal was to gather information from me regarding my relationship and marriage to Marlene Montgomery, formerly Marlene Fairchild; including the series of events that led to my divorce. He indicated that there would be several questions and he hoped it wouldn't be too intimidating or overly formal. His final advice was for me to try to relax and answer the questions to the best of my knowledge. He said he'd meet me at the address he provided for the attorney's office. The videotaped deposition took over two hours of painful memories, but the worst were still buried.

The light flashed red on the front of the recorder and the attorney began. "Good morning Mr. Fairchild."

"Good morning."

"The answer to these questions may be used in a trial and we'd like you to answer accurately. If you have any questions about my question, like you don't understand it or it's confusing, which is a good possibility," he flashed a smile before continuing, "or if you don't understand it for any other reason, you're welcome to ask me a question about what I'm asking. Do you have any questions before we get started?"

"No, I don't." As he requested, I gave my name and address for the record.

"What is your occupation?"

"I'm an advertising media executive."

"And what's your current marital status?"

"Married with three children."

He asked, "Were you formerly married to a Marlene Montgomery?"

"Well, when we first met, her last name was Allen. Her maiden name was Hughes. When we got married, she became Marlene Fairchild."

"How did you meet her?"

"She worked at the advertising agency where I was employed. She was there for about three months."

"Where did she go to school?"

"I think L.A. City College, but I'm not completely sure." He was moving through his questions fairly quickly and I was going deeper into my memories of her.

"And how long did you date, know, or associate with her, before you got married?"

"It was about a year and a half."

"When did you separate from her?"

"I was downsized, I mean, fired from my position. I got a new job with a company based in Chicago. We had a commuter marriage for about two years. But after eighteen months, I realized that she wasn't going to relocate."

"I'm handing you a copy of a divorce decree and I would like to have that marked Exhibit A. Do you recognize this document?"

I skimmed the document before answering, "Yes, I do."

"Does it appear to be the decree of dissolution that ended your marriage to Marlene Fairchild?"

"Yes, it does."

"Now, when you left for Chicago, did your wife go with you?"

"No. She remained in Los Angeles to care for her daughter who was seriously ill.

"How many children did she have?"

"To my understanding, two. One was supposed to be her nephew, Billy, who she said she and her first husband adopted. And her daughter's name is Sarah."

He had a perplexed look on his face. "I don't understand. She had somebody living with her? A nephew?"

"Yes. She told me they adopted him as a toddler and raised him as her son." I didn't go into detail about hiring a private detective to find out more.

"So did the two of you have much contact? How much contact did you have while you were in Chicago and she was in Los Angeles?"

"In the beginning, we had regular contact through phone calls, mail, trips home, and I sent money on a monthly basis for household expenses. She visited me in Chicago three times."

"Then how did things start to fall apart?"

"On her last visit, we looked at different places to live and hospitals for Sarah to continue her treatment. I came to the conclusion that we needed to merge households because it was becoming too costly to live apart. We actually found a place, so I leased it with an option to buy. But the day that I was moving from my corporate apartment to the new home, she called to tell me she wasn't coming."

"Uh-huh, I see. And what did you do as a result of that conversation?"

"Of course, it was devastating. I wouldn't have leased that big house if I felt she wasn't going to relocate. We had problems in our marriage in the past, but we were working towards getting together. So, her actions were surprising and hurtful."

"Was she employed in Los Angeles during that period?"

"When she worked, it was as a private duty nurse. I think she had the credentials of LPN, but I never actually saw her certificate."

"While you were separated, did you have any bank accounts together?"

"Yes, we did."

"Prior to your marriage, did she have any bank accounts on her own?"

"She was extremely private about her personal matters. I would imagine that she did, but I couldn't tell you which bank or what type of account."

"Did you set up your joint checking account after you got married?"

"Yes. Initially the arrangement was to give her money for household expenses. But after a while, that seemed to cause problems. It got so bad, I decided to seek counseling and she agreed. The counselor recommended that we handle all of our finances jointly; she felt that would give our marriage more stability. Taking the first step, I applied for a credit card for the both of us."

"Prior to the marriage, you didn't have any joint credit cards, did you?"

"No, none."

"Subsequent to the marriage, did she open any credit accounts other than the one Visa card you mentioned?"

"Well, yes she did. And I didn't know about many of them. I actually didn't find out about the cards until she sent me a batch of bills along with a note saying she could no longer handle the payments and she was sorry. Before I discovered my application was approved, she used the entire line of credit within the first month."

His eyebrows furrowed together, creating deeps lines. "How was all of this debt repaid?"

"By me, over many years after our separation and divorce. I had excellent credit when I married her, but my credit score was ruined for many years due to the excessive bills and living in two different states. A car repossession was on my report because of her, too."

"Did you give her authorization to open these accounts?"

"Absolutely not! The Visa card was the only one. I did put her name on my American Express card because I felt it could be controlled better since she knew the entire balance had to be paid every month."

"Reflecting back now, do you have any idea what she was using credit cards and cash advances for?"

"No. I mean when I confronted her, she would say she used the credit to pay bills, her past debt, and our current family debt. I discovered she was using the overdraft protection on the checking account with checks that were out of sequence; meaning checks from boxes not being used."

"Were these checks written on your account, your joint account or her account?"

"They were on my account."

"Your account?"

"Yes, mine."

"And had she signed the checks?"

"Yes."

"Did you authorize her to sign the checks?"

"No."

"You mentioned a repossession of a vehicle? Would you tell me about that?"

"Yes. I purchased the car for her on my credit. The purchase included her older car for trade-in value, which wasn't much since the car was eight years old. The new car was a two-year-old, low mileage Mercedes SL Model."

"Why was it repossessed?"

"It was my wife's car, so when I got my new position in Chicago, it stayed with her in Los Angeles. When she mailed all of her bills to me, the invoice for the car wasn't included. I assumed she was making the payment to Wells Fargo Bank. One day, I received a call from the bank stating that the payments were three months past due and they needed the account to be paid immediately. I explained my situation and the car was not in my possession. They informed me that the car was in my name so I was responsible for the debt. To make a long story short, I found out where the car was located and called the bank with the information. Marlene called me the next day asking about the car. This was the first time hearing from her in almost a year; I told her what happened and she hung up on me. I never heard from her again. A lawyer representing her called later that day and I referred her to my lawyer. An agreement was signed allowing her to pay off the debt and put the car in her name. I was notified that the car was paid off the following week, but the repossession remained on my credit report."

"Did you have any other knowledge of any attempts by her to use the name Fairchild before your marriage?"

"There was another time, but the store manager called me, so the credit wasn't granted. When I asked her about the situation, she claimed she didn't know anything about it."

"After your divorce, did she keep the name Fairchild?"

"I have no idea. But periodically, I receive applications for credit with Marlene Fairchild on it and this happened in Chicago and Atlanta."

"Did you see the name Montgomery on any of the applications?"

"No. Never."

"Lets return to an earlier statement. Marlene took checks from a new box instead of a checkbook?"

"Right."

"Did she sign your name on the checks or did she sign her own name?"

"She signed my name."

"Was it a habit during your marriage that she signed your name to documents?"

"No, no."

"Since your separation, has Marlene used your name or otherwise involved you in any of her financial dealings?"

"Not to my knowledge. Like I said, the last time I talked to her was in regards to the car. After that, I had my attorney work out the details with her lawyer."

"Did Marlene ever seem like she was hiding out from anybody or hiding from creditors?"

"No. The only incident that happened before we got married was when she approached me with some outstanding credit card bills she had during her first marriage. She explained that since she was dating me, he wasn't going the pay off the bills. They amounted to two or three thousand dollars and I helped her pay them off."

"This was during the beginning of the marriage?"

"It was right before we married."

"I see. Did she ever talk to you about the marriage itself and what she considered your marriage to be?"

"Our marriage?"

"Yes, Mr. Fairchild."

"Not really. I mean we had problems, mostly financial, but at times it was a very positive marriage. She was an excellent mother to Sarah and Billy and I got along well with the kids."

"So, did she ever tell you that your marriage was a marriage of convenience?"

"No. Never."

"Did she ever tell you that she married you because you were gay?"

At this point, I decided not to tell him about our sexual activities, I set my ego aside because God was working on me. "No. Why would she marry a gay person?"

"Maybe she wanted to help you out, give you some status."

"Something is very wrong with that woman!"

"Then if she said you're gay that would be a false statement?"

"She would definitely know that's a boldface lie."

"Okay. Was Marlene truthful with you during your marriage to her?"

"She used to embellish things. For example, she claimed to have a sister in Las Vegas who was actually Billy's birth mother. In over five years, I never saw or spoke to her. Billy was a really great kid and she never called, sent birthday cards or attended events like his high school graduation. I thought it was strange to have his real mother living so close; Los Angeles is an hour flight from Vegas. When I questioned Marlene about anything I thought was unusual, she got defensive and angry. So to keep the peace, I stopped asking questions."

"How about Billy's father? Did she mention anything about him?"

"Well, like I said, Billy was supposed to be the son of her phantom sister and she reacted badly when I asked questions about her, so I didn't dare ask about his father."

"Do you believe her dishonesty or hiding things about her personal affairs contributed to the breakdown of your marriage?"

"I think so. Initially, she had a valid reason not to relocate to Chicago because of Sarah's health. But after a while, I could sense she was hesitant about moving. She was born and raised in California and I'm sure she didn't want to leave her lifestyle there. But she kept going through the motions about joining me until she found someone that gave her a reason to stay in L.A. She probably knew long before that she was never going to leave California."

"How would you characterize your experience of Marlene regarding her honesty?"

"I don't feel she was ever completely forthright or honest with me. I'm not a psychologist, but I think she's emotionally unstable and a compulsive liar."

"How would you characterize your experience with Marlene regarding her integrity?"

"She wasn't someone that you could trust. She wasn't honest with me." I lowered my head, feeling ashamed that I allowed someone to get so close to my heart.

"Did she use any other names, to your knowledge, during your marriage?"

"Yes, she used her maiden name, Hughes, her last name with her first husband, Allen, and my last name."

"Okay. I have no further questions. Thank you, Mr. Fairchild."

The deposition concluded at eleven thirty that morning. I could tell that the attorney's objective was to establish the fact that Marlene was dishonest, misappropriated funds and lacked integrity. I noticed some of the questions were redundant to verify that my answers were consistent. That deposition ended my interaction with anyone involved in the case besides the attorney that sent a notarized copy of the deposition accompanied with a note that read,

James,

Here is a copy of your deposition transcript, for your records, as you requested. Thanks again for all of your HELP!

Russell Washington

An independent third party informed me that Dr. Montgomery was granted an annulment from his marriage to Marlene. The court found that prior and during the marriage, Marlene had stolen huge sums of funds from Dr. Montgomery and his partners. The court found that it was her intention to continue stealing and covering her tracks. They stated, it would be difficult to find a more egregious example of fraud than that case.

Those series of events were a horrible experience. We must always remember that in life's darkest moments, God is there to help us overcome any challenge and bring us closer to Him.

The Allure of a Predator

Chapter 12

Diagnosis and Prognosis

We hear so much in the media about predators but it's disheartening when the person you love, trust, and sleep next to is one. Marlene was diagnosed as a narcissist and she was undoubtedly a pathological liar. She was a compulsive spender who embezzled millions of dollars from her husband's medical practice. It didn't make sense that a successful entrepreneur, a well-educated media executive and a prominent medical doctor would marry and enable such a person. The answer is extremely complicated.

When I met Marlene, she seemed to be evolving into the person she would eventually become, but what I didn't consider at the time was that she was already that person. As a narcissist, she was conflicted between her false self versus her true self. I fell in love with a great, religious mother. She was an athlete who taught me how to play racquetball and her cooking and housekeeping skills were exceptional. Our intimate moments kept me longer than I should have stayed. Since I traveled frequently for work, it made it easier for her to keep up the false persona. However, when that changed, her true character began to surface. The vagueness about her past, compulsive lying and exhibition of manipulative behavior were all forewarnings. Her irresponsibility, impulsive spending, and violent behavior let me know that it was time to seek help. I felt there was hope for us because she agreed to participate in counseling and attend church services on a regular basis, but that was not enough. When a person is resistant and reluctant to change, they don't plan to take responsibility for their actions.

Shortly after my divorce from Marlene, my first wife revealed something I wish I had known. She told me that once my children returned home, they didn't want to visit me anymore. They felt that Marlene was disrespectful to their mother and questioned how I could have married such a poor excuse for a wife. Marlene even called my ex-wife in D.C. and told her my children should call me at the office, not at her house. I asked why she waited to tell me, but it was because she didn't think I would have believed her. She said at that point in my relationship, I thought Marlene could walk on water. Sadly, she was probably right. Red flags must not be ignored. If you know a person with these characteristics, they must not be overlooked. If you are exhibiting the aforementioned narcissistic traits, seek counseling immediately. If Marlene continued her therapy, she may have avoided the hardships she caused herself and the loved ones in her life.

Marlene's relationship and marriage to Dr. Montgomery was her narcissistic personality disorder on steroids. Dr. Montgomery later discovered that, with the authorization of a judge, she had their home phone tapped. As well, she convinced the accountant, from his former accounting firm, to help her commit fraud and embezzle funds. He believed he was married to a female psychopath and all I can say is, he was the doctor. His investigation into her background confirmed many things I felt, but couldn't always verify. Marlene was Billy's biological mother and Billy's father was a high school boyfriend who got Marlene pregnant when she was sixteen. The façade and lies she had to live with had an extremely negative impact on her emotional development. The doctor believed she had something to do with her first husband's death, but I don't think he had evidence of that.

Marlene's pattern of fraud when she embezzled funds over an eight-year period was controlled rather than erratic behavior. Her husband never would have had her working in his office handling the money if he knew her better and wasn't deceived. I could have predicted her willingness to steal from her own husband because she had the need, opportunity and rationalization to do so. She needed the cash to maintain her image of being independently wealthy. She handled the business operation at the doctor's office because the practice was doing so well, they didn't realize the theft was occurring over a long period of time. In the end, she was greedy and overconfident in her ability to prey on others.

You are not alone and help is available. In my case, God intervened. I was determined to make a marriage work at all cost and to my own detriment. I had one failed marriage and I felt another failed relationship was unacceptable. I continued to focus on the positives while ignoring the warning signs that were there to protect me. I tried to help my wife because I thought she was crying out for help, yet I realized that you cannot change people unless they are ready. The dilemma was my predator wife needed to accept her past and seek help to get beyond the pain. She was hurting but she didn't let God and a professional therapist help her true self have an opportunity to get well and heal. Dr. Charles Stanley said it best in his handbook, *Biblical Answers to Life's Tough Questions*. How can I confront a believer who has fallen spiritually?

"God gave Ezekiel a tremendous and ominous calling to confront His people about their sin. 'Son of man,' He told the prophet, cause Jerusalem to know her abominations. A tough calling! Even so, at times He will call us to do the same thing. So how can we manage it effectively?" (Ezekiel 16:2).

First, we must watch the spirit in which we confront the fallen one. We must be firm but gentle. We are to confront them "In a spirit of gentleness" (Galatians 6:1). Hurting people can be as fragile as glass; they don't need our condemnation. We don't go to them in anger or to vent. We go gently, remaining sensitive to their agony. We should not automatically interpret their inability to express grief as a lack of remorse or repentance. They may suffer so greatly that they can't get close to the physical tears for which their souls weep. We must remain firm in our efforts to bring the sin into the open, but we need to do so with gentleness and respect.

Second, we are to confront someone in the spirit of humility. "For if anyone thinks himself to be something, when he is nothing, he deceives himself" (Galatians 6:3). That way of thinking deeply offends God. Remember, we are all vulnerable to sin. "Considering yourself, lest you also be tempted"

(Galatians 6.1) means to examine ourselves with a sharp eye.

Lastly, we are to go in love, Galatians 6:2 uses a word that means "heavy burdens". We must go with the right spirit or we may as well not go at all. My spiritual immaturity hindered me in my quest to help Marlene. I did not confront her with a gentle or humble spirit and unfortunately, my love wasn't strong enough. It didn't matter how devoted I could have been because it was up to Marlene to acknowledge that she needed help. My intentions were good, but when I became an enabler to bad behavior, I became a part of the problem and not the solution.

It wasn't until after everything occurred that I wondered why the painting on her wall was so significant to her. Often, I'd return home and find her staring at it, deep in thought, as if she was fixated. The smile on her face seemed gratifying in some strange way, like the painting harbored a secret. Out of curiosity, I decided to do some research and found that Colchicum is a common flower, which grows naturally in gardens. However, it comes in different forms; the leaves and seeds are poisonous when ingested. Another name it is known by is "The Naked Lady" and its beauty disguises its deadliness, just like Marlene.

Marlene's alleged crimes and transgressions did not result in her serving time in prison or probation. I pray that she has asked God for forgiveness for her sins, her repentance has changed her conduct, and that she is now living an honest and productive life by giving all glory to God. I pray for her family and her victims.

Lord,

Life is sometimes difficult. We worry, we get weary and sometime we are heartbroken. But when we lift our eyes to You, Dear Lord, You strengthen us. When we are weak, you lift us up. Today and everyday we turn to You, Father, for our strength, for our hope, and for our salvation. Amen!

About the Author

Charles Richardson currently resides in Columbus, Ohio and is the President of CHR Marketing Consultants, LLC. He earned a Master of Science degree from Baruch College, City University New York. Charles is committed to both civic and community service and has served on many boards including the King Arts Complex and the Columbus Urban League. For more information, visit www.charleshrichardson.com

The Allure of a Predator

24728413R00165

Made in the USA
Middletown, DE
04 October 2015